This Thing Called Love

an Oyster Bay novel

Olivia Miles

~ Rosewood Press ~

This Thing Called Love

an Oyster Bay novel

Chapter One

The sun was just starting to set, casting a warm orange glow over the sky, when a gull swooped down over the Atlantic and, eliciting a shriek from a little girl in a crisp white cotton sundress, tore the remaining half of her sandwich right from her hand.

Hannah Donovan grabbed the camera that was hung around her neck most of her waking hours and quickly zoomed in for a shot, grinning when she pulled back from the lens a moment later to study the screen. Surprise, horror, and confusion were written all over the little girl's face. Scanning the beachfront, Hannah found the seagull resting on a rock, and she crouched down for a shot of the bird happily enjoying its dinner.

She could have stayed out here all evening, capturing still frames of life as it moved all around her, but she had somewhere to be, and, because recently she wasn't used to having to be anywhere, she was already half an hour late.

It was good to have structure, she reminded herself, as she closed her lens and dropped the camera back against her chest. It was good to start the day knowing what was planned for it, instead of roaming where the muse took her, never very certain of what tomorrow would bring. Sure, it had been a fun run, travelling around South America, with no agenda or timeline, her camera in her hand and the world at her fingertips, but that couldn't really last forever.

But then, nothing did.

Oops. There she went. Being cynical again. And she'd promised herself not to be, especially tonight, when everyone was gathering for her cousin Bridget's bridal shower. Tomorrow, yes, tomorrow she could be cynical, when she woke up in her childhood bed knowing that nothing had changed in all the years she had been gone, despite her efforts, but tonight she would be the perfect guest. She'd smile as the presents were opened, she'd drool over the diamond engagement ring, and she'd toast to love and happiness that would last a lifetime.

She snorted, then quickly gave herself a silent scolding. Not tonight. Tonight she would behave! After all, she'd agreed to photograph Bridget's wedding next weekend, which would be held at the Harper House Inn she now ran, and Hannah would do it properly.

But of course, that wasn't the only reason she was

back in town.

She hurried up the wooden steps that transported her from the sandy shore to the deck of the Oyster Bay Hotel, a large, lavish, crisp white building that was right in the center of town, that some said was one of the prettiest buildings in the state of Maine. The sprawling back porch rail was lined with strings of lights that glowed in the dusk, and despite her reservations about coming back to her hometown, Hannah felt her pulse skip with sudden excitement. Parties meant champagne and cake and laughter and fun. And she needed a little fun, darn it.

Soon she was at the top of the stairs, crossing the deck as she weaved her way through the café tables, where guests sat enjoying the view with their dinner, and pushed through the revolving doors into the lobby. She followed the signs to the Garden Terrace, where the invitation that had been e-mailed two weeks ago said the event would be held, and pulled open the door, surprised by the number of women who were gathered on the bluestone patio, surrounded by rose bushes in their second bloom.

She scanned the group, looking for Bridget, the guest of honor, but she froze in place when she spotted a different blonde-haired woman at the back of the room instead.

"Evie?" She blinked, trying to make sense of it. When she'd arrived at the house, there was no sign of life. Her plane was delayed and her dad was already at The

Lantern, the restaurant he'd run for her entire life. And he'd never said a word about her sister being here when she'd called last week, after deciding that really, now was the right time to come home. For a little while at least.

Unlike herself, Evie's expression registered no surprise. Her eyes were always a cool and steady blue, unlike Hannah's brown eyes that she'd inherited from her mother. The only thing she'd inherited from her mother, really. Well, other than the brown hair—and a really annoying habit of sneezing a dozen times in a row after having a good cry. Not that she'd ever seen her mother cry. But her half-sister Kelly did the same thing, and well, it didn't take a detective to put two and two together there.

Other than that, she and her mother were nothing alike, as Hannah had grown to discover, and eventually accept. Almost

To her credit, Evie leaned in for a hug, as casually as if they'd seen each other yesterday, not...well, Hannah had lost track of how long it had been. Years. Five years since she'd come back for a college graduation party for Evie. And who could forget that visit?

"Dad told me you were arriving this evening."

"Funny," Hannah said, the sarcasm in her tone a little thicker than she'd hoped. "He didn't tell me anything." She didn't know why this omission stung. It was a reminder, perhaps, of all the other things she and her family didn't share with each other. Her conversation with her father had been stilted and brief. Maybe he had been as uncomfortable as her. Maybe he was afraid that if he told her Evie was going to be here, she wouldn't come.

"Well, it was a last minute decision," Evie said with a shrug. She sipped her champagne, which was pink. Come to think of it, Hannah thought, looking around, everything was pink, even Evie's shawl that was draped over her shoulders.

She looked down at her own dress, which was not pink, remembering all at once that in addition to mentioning the Garden Terrace, the invitation had also stressed that guests should wear pink.

And she was wearing blue. Turquoise, actually, as luck would have it. Her favorite color.

Evie seemed to read her thoughts but didn't comment on them. "I'm staying at the house."

Just like told times then, Hannah thought, but then, those times had been good, happy, and solid. A lump rose in her throat when she thought of how much she'd had back then, and how much she'd thrown away in search of... what? Something better? Something more?

So much for that.

She looked at her sister, the sudden need to get back to that happier time and place burning strong. She opened her mouth, eager to apologize or explain or just communicate, because what they were doing now, standing here, having formal conversation like distant relatives, it wasn't right.

"Evie!"

Hannah turned in dismay to see her cousin Abby running toward them, and despite the ache in her chest, she couldn't help but grin. Abby's auburn hair bounced at her shoulders and the carnation-colored dress brought out the rosiness in her cheeks. Her eyes were always glimmering, and she pulled both sisters into a hug as she greeted them.

"My God, has Chip seen you both yet?" Abby's smile was radiant and so genuine that Hannah struggled to push back another wash of shame. As kids, the Harper cousins had been as close as her own sister once was, and their mother, Anne, had been like a surrogate, happy to include Hannah and Evie on back to school shopping trips in Portland, or invite them to bake cookies in their big kitchen at Christmas. Hannah had looked so forward to these days. Sure, their dad had tried, but there were gaps in his parenting that his sister had been able to fill. "It isn't right for young girls to grow up without a mother," she'd often hear her father mumble, and each time he said it, a part of her heart would break all over again and she'd had to resist yelling out that they did have a mother.

Just not one who lived with them anymore. Or visited. Or even called.

And so it was Anne who taught her how to apply makeup so she didn't look like she was trying too hard, and Anne who handed her tissues and bought her ice cream when her heart broke into a million pieces eleven years ago and she'd sworn she'd leave Oyster Bay and never come back.

But she had come back. Just a couple short years later, for Anne's funeral. Her husband's too. And later, for Evie's college graduation party.

Two short visits in all these years. And now, she was here indefinitely. Oy.

She glanced at Evie who seemed oblivious to the turmoil Hannah felt at being back here. But then, Evie hadn't gone so far away, and she had only just wrapped up grad school, having spent the last five years in Boston pursuing a dual master's program and some fancy internship. She was home, following the natural order of things, instead of scouring the world, searching for something that couldn't be found. Evie had always been that way. Content. Focused. Whereas Hannah...

"How long are you in town for?" Abby pressed, wedging herself in between them and linking their arms.

Hannah hesitated and looked over at Evie, surprised to see that she was doing the same. She opened her mouth to say something vague, but a woman Hannah remembered as the town busybody was already running toward them, or waddling, given the awkward knee-hugging length of her fuchsia colored skirt.

"Well, if it isn't the Donovan sisters! Home at long last!" Her eyes darted from Hannah to Evie and back again, and Hannah felt Abby nudge her with her hip. "It's a shame you girls couldn't attend Margo's wedding last spring, but then, of course, you're young and busy." The last word was spoken with a narrowing of the eye and a pinch of the lip.

"Margo understood, Dottie," Abby said with forced patience. "It wasn't a formal event and they planned it so quickly."

"So quickly that a few of us ladies were taking bets on baby names," Dottie continued with a waggle of the eyebrows. "But then, well, she's over there on her second glass of champagne, so I suppose we'll just have to wait a little longer!"

Abby gave a polite smile and said nothing else.

"And of course Bridget wasted no time either. After all, Jack just moved to town a few months ago and already they're tying the knot!"

"Life is short. Why wait?" Hannah said, rising to her cousin's defense. After a lousy first marriage and a bad divorce, Bridget deserved all the happiness she could find. If it lasted...

Well, snap. There she went again.

Now Dottie's eyes sparked. "Why wait, indeed? So does that mean you have someone special in your life?" Her eyes flitted, eventually landing on Evie, when Hannah said nothing.

"Me?" Evie coughed on her drink. "No, I've been too busy with school."

"Of course. You always were such a bookworm. No, I meant Hannah, of course." Dottie shook her head as Evie's mouth drooped into a deep frown and she studied her glass.

Oh, no. Hannah felt half a dozen eyes swivel and

fixate on her as she opened her mouth and then closed it again.

"Happily single," she said.

"Oh, now," Dottie chided. "No use trying to make light of a tough situation. I happen to know several eligible men who would just love to take a pretty girl like you out to dinner."

Hannah felt her back teeth graze as her smile began to droop.

"After all, you don't want to attend Bridget's wedding without a date, do you?"

"I'm happy being alone," she replied, but the little tug in her chest said otherwise.

"Don't be silly, my dear. No one is happy being alone. Well, maybe Evie is, but she has her work and studies." Dottie smiled, but Evie seemed to blink in confusion. "You just give me your number, Hannah, and I'll make a few calls. Or, are you staying with your father? Perfect, he's in the book."

Hannah glanced at Abby, who explained, "The phone book."

Ah. Of course. Hannah made a mental note to call the phone company and have her father's number permanently changed and marked as unlisted.

"I encouraged your cousin Margo to give that Eddie Boyd a second chance and look at her now," Dottie added. "Well, still not pregnant, but any day, I'm sure!"

"Speaking of Margo," Abby said as she steered them

away, somewhat less than subtly. When they were only slightly out of earshot, she rolled her eyes and said, "Honestly! I'm just glad I'm in a serious relationship or it would be me she'd be trying to set up with every Tom, Dick, and…Margo!"

Margo turned at the sound of her name, and a big smile spread across her face faster than she could run over to greet the sisters. "I was just about to save you from Dottie. Don't tell me she's already giving you the lowdown on the town gossip?"

"Worse," Hannah said. "She's thinking of eligible men to set me up with. Apparently it's not acceptable for me to attend Bridget's wedding stag."

"I'm going stag," Evie pointed out.

"Perfect, you can go together!" Margo said good-naturedly, but Hannah felt uneasy. She and Evie hadn't been alone together in a long time, and the last time they'd seen each other, they'd fought.

"Besides," Margo continued, with a conspiratorial wink. "You never know who you might end up meeting at the wedding. I happen to know a few single men on the invitation list."

Hannah stifled a groan and, eyeing a waiter with a tray of champagne flutes over near the back of the room, made a polite excuse to get herself a refreshment.

She took a glass, then, muttering something about bringing another for her sister, she double-fisted her way around the perimeter of the garden, until she was hovering near the edge, in the doorway to the lobby.

There was no use feeling sorry for herself. She couldn't afford to feel sorry for herself. She was broke. She'd run through her savings traipsing around South America, under the guise of a "sabbatical," when really, she'd been fired from her job at the fashion magazine and was all too happy to leave the West Coast behind her, and not just because of her disgraced career.

And now she was in her hometown. Broke. Unemployed. Drowning her sorrows in a bubbly pink drink, for God's sake. But it didn't ease the hole in her heart of the loss she felt when she thought of what had led her to the California.

Or who she'd left behind.

*

Evie tried to admire the beautiful diamond engagement ring that hugged her cousin Bridget's left ring finger. She tried to admire sweet little Emma's pink party dress. She even tried to smile politely when Dottie interrupted the group again to inquire not so subtly how Ryan felt about Bridget remarrying "after all this time."

But then, that's what Evie did. Evie always did what she should do. It made no sense, and went against research findings. After all, hadn't she learned in her psychology classes that birth order played a significant role in defining personality traits? Oldest children tended to be more organized, responsible, time sensitive, and conscientious. But Hannah was none of those things and

Evie was all of them. It was Evie who would do the laundry and fold the clothes each Sunday, once she was big enough. It was Evie who would make not only her bed but her sister's, even if their dad hadn't really cared about that type of thing. When he forgot to pick her up from piano practice one night, she used her allowance money to buy a weekly calendar that she hung on the fridge, where she wrote in all of her activities and her sister's, so that Chip could keep them straight. And speaking of piano, she practiced every day, without any prodding. Hannah, on the other hand, had abandoned the guitar less than three months after receiving it for Christmas when she was ten. Even at the tender age of eight, Evie had known that would happen.

She'd always been a keen observer of human behavior, always been fascinated by it, really. It was why she'd become a licensed therapist. But it didn't take her shiny new degree to realize that something was bugging Hannah. And because she was her sister, she should really do the right thing and track her down and figure out what it was.

Sometimes, though, she was just plain tired of doing what she should do.

"So what are you going to do now that you've graduated?" Margo asked innocently enough, not realizing that this very question kept Evie up all night, and recently, had started to give her hives.

She had heard about people who broke out in hives from stress, finding it just plain odd, really. When exams came up, she sometimes lost her appetite, but hives?

But sure enough, now her cheeks were starting to itch and she could probably count to ten before the rash broke out.

"Your dad mentioned something about working in a hospital in Boston?" Bridget added, as she frowned at Emma, who was reaching for yet another glass of punch from a tray that was being passed around. "It's getting late and you have camp tomorrow." She sighed and looked back at the women. "I knew it was crazy to have this on a Sunday night, but the inn was full last night and I hated to turn away the business."

The hospital in Boston. Yes, that had been the plan. Had being in the past tense. As in, not going to happen. And she'd been confident enough that her flawless GPA and the hours upon hours she had spent devoting herself to her studies and clinical hours at the sacrifice of all else would guarantee her a prominent position. That success led to more success. Instead, it seemed that she wasn't well-rounded enough. And no, piano didn't count. She'd asked. They wanted someone with more life experience. Meaning someone who was part of clubs and organizations and understood teamwork and leadership. Things she hadn't made time for…because she had been so busy studying!

Oh no, now her scalp was starting to itch and she could tell that little Emma was on to her. Children were keen that way, and despite being only nine, Evie could tell that her first cousin once removed was a smart little girl. Sharp and sensitive and creative, too. And she played the piano! My, they had a lot in common. Evie's eyes narrowed. She'd have to have a talk with Bridget. Warn her about getting Emma in extras. That good grades weren't always enough. Clubs. Yes, clubs were the key. And team sports. Who knew?

"That didn't work out…" She itched her cheek. Then her other cheek. And that little spot above her eyebrow where they always grew the biggest.

"Excuse me for a minute. The bathroom is…"

"That way," Bridget pointed sharply toward the double French doors that led to the lobby, and Evie fled, leaving behind her wide-eyed cousins who were no doubt talking about her right now.

She burst out into the lobby and right into Hannah, who was holding a glass of champagne with her left hand, while she drained the one in her right.

The expression on her sister's face transformed from guilt to horror, confirming Evie's worst suspicions. "What the hell happened to your face?" she exclaimed.

Evie skirted her eyes to the left. Luckily, the pianist at the baby grand near the bar had drowned out the accusation. "I'm having a reaction to all those roses out there," she fibbed.

Hannah looked at her skeptically. "I thought you liked roses."

"I do. I did. I mean, I do." Oh no, they were starting to spread down her neck. She could follow the tingle.

Soon they would be covering her collarbone. "I should go to the bathroom."

"Cold water isn't going to help you now," Hannah remarked. Always helpful, her sister was. "Here," she said, handing her the remaining glass of champagne.

"I already have a glass," Evie said, holding up a hand. It was nearly full, and she'd been holding onto it for nearly an hour. It went right to her head. And who needed that? She wanted to wake up tomorrow feeling refreshed and ready to...plan. Yes, to plan out her future. Now that her other plans had gone bust.

She suddenly realized that Hannah had never answered Abby's question. "How long are you here for?"

Hannah chewed her lip for a moment. Something she only ever did when she was trying to think her way out of something. "I don't know," she finally said.

Evie felt one of her swollen eyebrows hitch in surprise, and she quickly excused herself to the bathroom as she began clawing at the skin of her neck.

So Hannah was back in town without a plan in place? Well, well. After all these years, it seemed the sisters had something in common then.

Chapter Two

At seven sharp on Monday morning, Dan Fletcher took a long swig of coffee from his thermos and set it back in the cup holder as he drove around the cedar-shingled house and pulled to a stop outside the detached garage, where he'd have easy access to the kitchen entrance.

He checked his cell phone, by habit, not because he expected there to be any new messages from Lucy. Not at this hour, when she still asleep. Not at any hour, if he was being honest with himself. When he'd bought her that cell phone for her tenth birthday this winter, he'd assumed it would be a good way for them to keep in touch when he was out on a job site. Instead, she spent more time than usual locked in her room, chatting with her friends. No, not chatting. Texting. Kids didn't talk anymore these days. At least his kid didn't talk to him.

Not the way she used to, at least. Once, she used to share every detail of her day. It would come out in a crazy rush the moment he picked her up from school. Sometimes he felt dizzy with the way she bounced around, subject to subject, barely taking a breath. Now, he had to ask questions. And even then, he didn't always get an answer. Especially when it stirred up something to do with her mother.

He huffed out a sigh and pushed open the door, dust kicking up in the warm salty breeze as his boots hit the gravel. It was demolition day, a hot, humid day for it, but he'd known worse.

Chip Donovan had told him to let himself in, that he'd be at the restaurant at the crack of dawn to take in the produce deliveries for the day and make a stop at the harbor for fresh catch. Sure enough, it was barely past seven and the door was unlocked, the kitchen so quiet when he walked inside that the floorboards creaked beneath him.

Usually he'd line the planks with paper, keep the dust out, but this was a full gut job, right down to shiny new hickory floors. Something Chip had waited a long time to do, considering he was a man who liked to cook.

With a look around, Dan realized the place was in even worse shape than he'd remembered. Not that he'd been here often, only to discuss the details of the renovation with Chip about six weeks ago. Now, alone in the room, he dared to let his gaze roam to the built-in eating nook, with the bench that lined the bay window, a small smile forming at his mouth as quickly as it fell.

Those days were long behind him now, and he'd made peace with that. He had a daughter to focus on now. Even if that daughter didn't even text him, much less speak to him as much as he'd have liked.

With that, he turned, walked out the door and propped it open with a rock he pulled from the garden hedge, and started unloading his truck. He'd knock out the upper cabinets today, maybe even get to the counters. The appliances would be replaced, but Chip wanted to keep the fridge for the renovation process so he didn't have to eat every meal at The Lantern.

Sweat ran from his forehead before he'd even had a chance to pick up his sledgehammer, and on his last trip to the truck, he took off his flannel and tossed it in the front seat. Chip never had gotten around to installing central air in the old house, and the window unit would only help so much.

Still. Sometimes you just had to make the best of what you had.

Or so he'd been telling himself for the last eleven years.

With his toolbox in hand, he shut the back of the truck and turned to the house, and that was when he saw her. The dark hair and eyes that he'd almost dared to forget, and for a second, he wondered if his mind was playing tricks. But the heat wasn't that bad, not yet anyway, and this was still her home, even if she never visited.

He hesitated, considered hopping in the truck and peeling off down the driveway; he'd tell Chip he'd have to find another man for the job. A man who wasn't haunted by the complications of his past he couldn't quite call a mistake. Could never call a mistake, really.

But his equipment was in the house and time had passed and this day was bound to happen eventually.

With a slow grin he walked over to the open door and leaned against the jamb. "Well, look who's back," he said.

*

Hannah had played out this scenario a hundred times over the years. A thousand times, really. In her mind, when she saw Danny again, she'd be on the arm of a very handsome man. Someone infinitely more handsome than Danny, with his chiseled jaw and strong, straight nose, and those deep-set eyes...

Right, back on track. In her mind, she would be wearing something fabulous, not the cut-off shorts and tee shirt she was currently wearing. And her hair would be brushed. Yeah, tangled hair had never been part of the fantasy. And she'd for sure have a rock solid career to brag about. And she'd see Danny and she'd feel nothing. Absolutely nothing. And she'd smile a breezy smile and maybe even give him an air kiss or two as if all this were ancient history and really, she barely even thought about it, so engrossed was she in her new and better and fulfilling life.

But this scenario wasn't unfolding at all. And that breezy attitude she'd hoped for? Forget that. Her knees were shaking, her heart was doing jumping jacks, and her stomach felt funny, as in, might get sick at any moment type of funny. Meaning, not so funny at all.

"What are you doing here?" Not exactly the most witty comment, but the best she could come up with at the moment.

He held up a toolbox, his biceps flexing under the pull of his tight white tee shirt. "Redoing your dad's kitchen."

She blinked, trying to process what this implied. "You mean, you come here every day?"

He chuckled under his breath as he walked up the step and into the kitchen. He set the toolbox down with a thud. "I will be here every day. I start today."

"For how long?" She hoped he couldn't hear the panic in her voice. It was hard enough being back here, knowing he was looming somewhere in town, that she'd have to keep her guard up and her eyes wide. But this... well, this was laughable.

If she had money in the bank she'd board the very next flight out of here. But she didn't. Just like she didn't have money for a hotel.

He shrugged, pulled out a crow bar. "Four weeks should do it."

"Four—" She couldn't even bring herself to say the word. Weeks, not days, and days would have been hard enough.

"How long are you in town for?" He glanced at her, his blue eyes deep and earnest, and a pain cut right through her chest.

She looked away. "Not sure of my plans at the moment. I'm in town for Bridget's wedding." She didn't mention that she would have had to come back anyway, given her situation.

"I'll be at the wedding too," he said, their eyes locking for one knowing second. This was it. They'd managed not to see each other for over eleven years and now, well, now there was no avoiding it.

Well, not if she could help it.

She backed up, creating as much space between them as she could, until her back hit the fridge, and she was forced to stop.

"Well, I should go. I have, um...to go."

Graceful exit if ever there was one. She had been planning to leave out the kitchen door but instead turned and walked back down the hall to the front door, where she stood on the stoop, heart pounding, and wondered just what she was going to do next, because by her calculation, she couldn't return again until at least five o'clock.

Her hair wasn't brushed and cut-off jean shorts were too casual for pounding the pavement, looking for gainful employment. But none of that mattered.

What mattered was getting out of this house. Away from Dan. And all the memories he still stirred up.

With that, she grabbed her camera from the front hall table and ran out the front door. She'd walk to town. And she'd stay there all day. Until Dan was gone.

Again.

*

Instead of walking to town, Hannah walked along the beach, until she finally came upon the big, white Victorian house that was once the Harper cousins' house and was now Bridget's inn.

She walked up the porch stairs and around to the back of the deck, where a woman sat at a table, overlooking the stretch of grass that met the ocean.

"Mimi!" Hannah smiled at the elderly woman who was the closest thing to a grandmother she'd ever known. While she was technically the Harper sisters' paternal grandmother, none of them had known their shared set of grandparents, and Hannah knew even less of her mother's family than she did of her mother.

"Evie?" Mimi frowned at her, as if trying to place her, and Hannah had the horrible, uneasy reminder of how much time had passed, and how much could transpire in that time.

"It's Hannah," she said, coming to sit in the chair beside Mimi, whose face was thinner and whose hair was whiter than she remembered. "I heard you got married."

Another wedding she had missed, but then, she supposed she had lost count of all the little celebrations she hadn't been a part of.

"Yes, I did get married. And that's why I'm here."
Mimi folded her hands in her lap and stared at Hannah
expectantly. "Earl and I aren't on the same schedule. I'm
up early and he's up late. I used to meet the girls for
dinner sometimes. They'd take me to The Lantern. They
know how much I love Chip's twice-baked potatoes."
Here she smiled, and Hannah did too. They had a shared
history. A shared familiarity. A shared sense of place.
How long had it been since she could talk to someone—
anyone—like this?

Everything in California had felt foreign and unnatural.
She could still remember the first week she'd gone to live
with her mother, when college was over and the dorm
had kicked her out, how she felt like a stranger, uncertain
of their ways, felt empty when Kelly referred to their
routine or their traditions or their holidays.

It had been different when she was still in school, only
visiting her mother, not living with her. Then she had an
excuse for feeling like an outsider. But under her roof,
there were no more excuses. They were all a family. And
she was not part of it.

"I do love my father's twice-baked potatoes," Hannah
said. She hadn't been to the restaurant in so long, but
now, just thinking about her father's recipes made her
mouth water. She'd go there later today. Maybe see about
a part-time job, like she'd done back in high school.

"They're divine," Mimi sighed. "But now I come here
some mornings instead of going to dinner. Earl doesn't

even notice. That man can *snore!*" She pinched her lips
and shuddered, and Hannah burst out laughing.

The kitchen door opened and Abby came out with a
tray of scones that she set on the table. "Well, this is a
surprise! I'll bring another plate. Coffee too?"

Hannah nodded. "Please."

Abby returned quickly, and Hannah motioned to the
extra chair. "Sit with us?"

"I'm on duty and there are still guests in the dining
room. But I'll come out when I'm wrapped up. And I'll
bring you today's special."

Hannah shook her head as Abby disappeared again.
"She's all grown up." Although, considering they were
roughly the same age, she could say the same for herself.
Maybe.

"About time!" Mimi said. "That girl was starting to
worry me."

Hannah just smiled and took a sip of her coffee. The
scones smelled delicious, and she happily broke a piece
off one and ate it. "Wow. Abby made these?"

"I taught her everything she knows, but you don't see
me asking for any credit around here," Mimi said, primly
reaching for her own coffee mug.

Hannah hid her smile behind the rim of her cup. "So
where are Bridget and Jack? And Emma?"

"Emma has camp in the summer," Mimi said. "Bridget
is probably getting her ready now. I wouldn't go in there
just now. Mornings are very stressful for Bridget with the
guests coming down and the little one needing to get

ready. My head about spun around last time I entered that kitchen at breakfast hour."

"Well, I'm perfectly happy sitting out here," Hannah said, as she settled back against her chair. There was a view of the sea, as far as the eye could take her, and if she looked far enough, she could see sailboats bobbing on the waves.

"Your father happy to have you back?" Mimi asked sharply.

"What?" Hannah felt herself stiffen. "I...I haven't had much chance to see him last night. I arrived last night and then he was already gone this morning."

"Stop by his restaurant then." Mimi paused. "After you've brushed that hair."

Hannah looked out onto the ocean again, self-consciously smoothing her hair. Yes, she supposed she would. She'd ask about a job. And...feel things out between them.

"Why so glum?" Abby asked as she returned again, this time holding two plates. "Vegetable quiche and a fresh salad, all made with produce fresh from the garden." She grinned as she proudly pointed to the patch of grass that had been torn away to make room for what was truly a flourishing garden.

"These tomatoes are beautiful," Hannah said, looking from her plate to the plants that were bursting with fruit. "I'm so impressed with you, Abby."

"I could say the same!" Abby grinned. "Heard you had a job at a fancy fashion magazine."

"Had," Hannah said with a pang of regret. "Had a job."

"Had?" Mimi cried. "You mean they fired you?"

"Not exactly fired," Hannah said, but who was she kidding? She had been fired. Fair and square, her dignity stripped from her as she sat before her boss, a petite woman with a severe bun who went by the name Char, and her twenty-two-year-old replacement. Whom she'd trained. Thinking she was going to be her assistant. She nearly laughed out loud over that, if she hadn't also wanted to cry. The plan had, embarrassingly, been in place for quite some time, and all that while, Hannah had grown more comfortable, more relaxed, more full of herself, really.

She was good at her job. Damn good. And so she dug her heels in a big way when she wanted a certain shot in the spread. Where had that gotten her? Sacked, penniless, and back in Oyster Bay shooting scenery. She'd given over six years to that magazine, working her way up from intern to assistant, and she cared. Maybe, she realized, looking back, she'd cared too much.

About a lot of things.

"Well!" Mimi's lips pinched so deep that they seemed to retract into her face. "Back in my day a person was appreciative to have steady work. But then, back in my day, women didn't work outside the home either. Women got married. Raised a family." She lifted an eyebrow and let her cool gaze shift from Hannah to Abby, who was rolling her eyes skyward.

"Duty calls!" Abby said, and then disappeared into the inn.

Mimi caught her eye. "She ditched you."

Hannah blinked, and then burst out laughing. "You always were a sharp one," she said, wagging her finger at Mimi. She could still remember the side-eye look Mimi had given her at a family picnic one of her last summers here, when she'd claimed a stomach ache but really wanted to run off to meet Danny. Nothing slid past her.

"So no love in your life at the moment?" Mimi asked, her tone considerably more subdued.

Hannah sighed, trying to push out the memory of seeing Danny this morning. He looked the same, minus a few wrinkles around his eyes, and she wasn't sure what she should have expected. Somehow it hurt her more to see how little he had changed. It made it feel like everything could just go back to the way it had once been between them.

She cut into her food, which was just as delicious as it looked. Abby had found her passion and calling right here in this small, remote town. Maybe there was hope for her, too.

"I'm focusing on my career for now," she said to Mimi, anticipating another lecture.

But Mimi just shrugged and picked up her fork. "There happens to be a fine-looking male nurse at

Serenity Hills. Abby was crushing on him for a while, but now she's back with Zach, as I'm sure you've heard."

Yes, Hannah had. "Thanks for the suggestion, but I'm okay on my own for now."

It was better that way. Easier. When you were alone, you could control today, and tomorrow. But when you tried to connect with someone, anything was possible. And it wasn't always something good.

"I'm trying to keep things...predictable for now."

"And you're saying that marriage is unpredictable?" Mimi looked at her like she was crazy. "There is nothing unpredictable when it comes to Earl's snoring! Or his routine! Or the fact that when I leave here today, he will look at me with a smile in his eyes and ask to take a walk in the rose garden. Same as every day." Mimi smiled, and for a moment, Hannah was almost convinced that for some people, at least, love might actually last.

They sat chatting until they'd finished their meals, talking about Emma and the upcoming wedding, and the suit that Mimi intended to wear, even though all her granddaughters insisted she would overheat.

And then Mimi went inside to fetch Bridget for a ride back to the nursing home where she now lived, and Abby emerged with a conspiratorial wink.

"I'll give you a lift back into town."

Relieved not to have to walk all that distance, Hannah followed Abby out the back door and onto the gravel drive, looking for a car. Instead, Abby casually pulled a pale blue bike from the side of the fence and grinned at her.

"Wait," Hannah said. "I thought you said you would give me a lift."

Abby patted the seat. "Room for both of us, and I can always stand. Don't you remember how we would always do this when we were little?"

"Little, yes. And much, um, smaller." Hannah calculated how long it would take her to walk to town. What else did she have to do with her time?

"It'll be fine. Get on," Abby said. She waited, showing no signs of giving up.

With a sigh, Hannah swung her camera strap around so her camera hit the middle of her back and positioned herself at the rear end of the banana-shaped seat. Abby climbed on, pedaling a little unsteadily as they made their way down the drive, and Hannah gripped the seat with one hand and Abby with the other, thinking that really, this was a very ridiculous idea.

"We're too old for this," she said, as Abby hit a rock and they nearly fell into the grass.

"Just let me get on the main road and then it will be easier," Abby insisted, as she pedaled a little harder.

She made a shaky turn to the left and then they were off, down the road, Abby's auburn hair whipping in Hannah's face, like two eight-year-olds, out for some afternoon shenanigans. Like it used to be. Like it could have maybe always been, if Hannah hadn't left.

They hit a bump, and Hannah felt her body lift in the air and come back down on the seat with a thud. Abby flashed her a wide-eyed look over her shoulder and cracked a rueful smile. And Hannah laughed. She laughed and laughed the way she hadn't laughed since she'd left Oyster Bay and everyone who had once meant everything.

Chapter Three

Evie stood at the hostess stand of The Lantern, telling herself that it beat helping out in the kitchen, even though that did little to solace her. She told herself that she was doing her dad a favor, rolling up her sleeves and helping out and all that, but this, too, failed to convince her.

Who was she kidding? She was a terrible therapist. She couldn't even cheer up herself!

"My bartender called in sick," her dad said, coming out of the kitchen and motioning to the empty space at the front of the room. "Want to cover his shift? Laurie can take over here for the afternoon."

Evie eyed the gleaming bar with the glass bottles stacked behind it in neat rows, anchored by two weathered life preservers that had been part of the décor since Evie could remember. She barely knew how to make a margarita, much less anything more complicated, but it would be more stimulating than smiling at tourists and the locals who were filtering in for their lunch break, and so, rather impulsively, and certainly not characteristically, she said, "Yes!"

"Thanks for helping out," her dad said as she followed him to the bar.

She gave a sad smile, suddenly worried that if she looked into his kind blue eyes she might just burst into tears here and now. He was helping her out, and he knew it. He'd always been thoughtful that way. Careful with his questions. Gentle with his words. Sensitive with his heart.

And Hannah had thrown that all back at him, hadn't she? Chasing after their mother the first chance she had, turning her back on the family that had been there, day in and day out, not the one who had run off, barely to be heard from again.

She was getting angry again. Seeing Hannah last night had fired her up, just as she knew it would. But as much as she was angry toward her sister for her betrayal, a part of her also understood, and pitied her for it. Hannah wanted to know their mother. It was a natural need. And no doubt she had been disappointed by the outcome.

"Glasses are here and bottle opener is over there." Chip quickly picked up a few gadgets and pointed at a few mixers. Evie suddenly had a newfound reason for cursing her lack of social life during college and grad school. The most she ever drank was a white wine or the occasional glass of champagne, and even then, she never finished the glass.

"Don't worry." Her dad grinned, no doubt seeing the panic in her face. "The guys who sit at the bar order beers. We've got three on tap and the rest in fridge." He tapped the small appliance underneath the counter.

She blew out a breath, feeling a little better. She could handle pouring a beer. Besides, it was a Monday. And it wasn't even noon. How many people would sit at the bar?

Quite a few, she realized, within about ten minutes.

The first guy said he was waiting for a friend and positioned himself at the end of the bar, eventually asking for a Bud Light. Easy. The next customer was the friend, an attractive woman that Evie assumed was renting one of the expensive summer houses out near Gull Point, based on the crisp white cigarette pants and halter top, and the hint of a Boston accent. When she ordered a glass of Cabernet, Evie had to press her mouth together as she uncorked the bottle, thinking how one drop would ruin that pristine outfit.

The first guy worked down at the docks. She recognized the look, knew it from growing up here. Too much sun on the arms and face, a visor that did little to ward off skin cancer, cargo shorts paired with industrial shoes. Calloused fingers.

She stared at him in borderline fear, hoping to God he stayed true to his stereotype and didn't go ordering some frilly drink like a daiquiri.

"Whatever's on tap," he said, glancing at a menu.

Oh, sweet relief. She picked up a glass and stared at the taps, suddenly remembering that there were three and knowing she wouldn't be able to describe any of them. She glanced back, but he seemed disinterested and just happy for the air-conditioning, so she pulled the middle tap and filled the glass before hesitantly sliding it along the counter.

"Anything else?"

The man set down the menu and tented his hands, releasing a deep sigh. He looked up at her through clear green eyes that were a sharp contrast to his tanned skin. "You know what I really need?"

She blinked, expecting him to say a hamburger or a lobster roll. Instead he said, "I need a new wife."

She stared at him, wondering if he was just having some fun with her. But he shook his head and said, "Seems that Jill has been getting busy with Dave in the boathouse." He slurped his beer until half of it was gone. "Seems they've been waiting until I'm out on the boats, when they figure they have a solid hour before I'll be back."

Evie glanced at the door, wondering if another customer might come in and save her. "Oh my," she said politely.

He shook his finger at her, a sly smile pulling at his mouth. "But they calculated wrong."

She bit back a sigh, then thought, oh, what the hell? "And how did they manage to do that?"

By the time he'd polished off his beer and started

another, Evie learned that Ron had been married for eight years and suspected that his wife was cheating on him for seven. His proof hadn't come until this past weekend, when he'd forgotten some rope at the boathouse and made an impromptu stop. While his suspicions were validated, he was devastated, but he had thrown a good punch at his coworker, even if he'd missed, tripped over the rope that was tangled on the floor, and ended up with a fishing net on his head.

"Evie?"

Evie looked up to see her sister staring at her in confusion. Evie was suddenly zapped back to reality, to the fact that she wasn't a bartender at all, and that she didn't even like to drink, and that she was out of her element and that it was obvious.

She hadn't seen her sister since she'd excused herself to the bathroom last night. She'd made an early exit after that, taken a cold shower and some anti-histamines, and put herself to bed. But she hadn't slept. Instead she'd lain awake, staring at the ceiling, feeling the fresh salty air blow in through the open window, wondering what the hell she was going to do with her life.

Hannah was staring at her, and another customer was asking about a refill. Evie grinned apologetically at the poor man, but he just grinned and slapped a twenty on the table, a generous tip was clearly included. "You've been a lot of help," he said, nodding. "A lot of help. I really appreciate you listening."

"My pleasure," Evie said, realizing, with a strange sensation, that it was. It wasn't exactly the psychiatric ward of one of New England's most prestigious hospitals, but it was…something.

*

So Evie was working at The Lantern. Meaning she'd beat her to the job. No wonder the house had been so quiet when she'd woken. Evie must have hitched a ride into town with their father. Hannah mentally scratched that job option from her list, even though she was sure that, if asked, her dad would happily find space for her in the restaurant, too.

Did Evie even know how to mix a martini? If so, she'd changed quite a bit in the few years since they'd last seen each other.

"Are you working here now?"

Evie's face grew red. "Just until I land somewhere permanently. School just finished, so…" Evie wiped down the bar with a rag, and Hannah dropped onto a stool. "You looking for Dad?"

"I was…" Not that it would do much good. Or change matters. She leaned into her elbows, lowering her voice, even though the din from the restaurant was loud. "I didn't realize that Dad was redoing his kitchen."

"Oh, he didn't warn you about that?" Evie winced. "Not exactly the best time to decide to come home."

Her smile was pleasant, and Hannah had to tell herself firmly not to read anything into the words. It was guilt talking, her own guilt, because God knew her father had never said a single word to make her feel bad for going off in search of her mother after college and not visiting much since then either. But Evie...Evie hadn't been so tight-lipped.

The last time she'd come back to town she'd sat in this very restaurant, where Chip was hosting Evie's college graduation party. Evie had a bright future ahead of her, of course, one with a concrete plan of action. Whereas Hannah...well, Hannah was floundering. She had spent years trying to forge a relationship with her mother and failing miserably. Her mother was aloof, distant, and seemed downright uncomfortable around her, as if she was a reminder of a part of her life she didn't want to remember. Hannah had a low-paying job as a photographer's assistant at the magazine. She was sharing a room with her half-sister Kelly who was halfway through college and still living at home. She didn't know what she was doing. She didn't feel at home there. But she didn't feel at home here either.

She sat at the bar, nursing a glass of wine, feeling out of place and twitchy, smiling politely when people asked questions about her life in California, putting a rosy spin on a situation that was so far from ideal it was almost laughable, if it didn't make her cry.

She'd been working up the courage to come back, to admit defeat, but she just couldn't.

Back then she still had hope. Back then, she wasn't

willing to give up on it just yet.

Evie had asked all the normal questions, and Hannah had misread this as a sign that maybe Evie had come around to the situation, that maybe she was okay with Hannah being on the West Coast. So she'd latched onto the one bearable part of it all: their sister. Immediately, she'd known she'd made a mistake.

"So you're trading us for them then, huh?" Evie had accused, with fire and hurt in her eyes.

"It's not like that," Hannah had insisted. "I'm just getting to know them. They're your family, too."

"My family is right here. In Oyster Bay," Evie had said firmly. "So you're staying out there?"

"Well, I have a job there," Hannah said slowly.

The answer didn't suffice. "So we're not good enough for you then? All those years, all those days. All the holidays. All the times you were sick. None of it mattered?"

"Evie—"

"She wasn't there for any of it," Evie said, her voice rising in a way that Hannah wasn't used to. Usually Evie was calm, measured. Hannah realized then that it was the first time her sister had ever been angry with her. Really, truly angry. And worse, hurt.

Only Hannah hurt too. "I don't see why you can't understand, seeing that you plan on becoming a therapist and all that. Aren't you supposed to be in better touch with people's emotions?"

It was a low blow, but Evie had hit a nerve. She'd

tapped into her worst fears. Her guilt. And her doubt for pursuing something that she probably should have left alone. Their mother had run off on them. She hadn't been a part of their lives. Who was Hannah to try to chase someone who didn't want to be found?

"I understand emotion. And behavior. And I know that you hurt a lot of people here, Hannah, even if they'd never tell you so. But I'm telling you. I hope it was worth it to you. I hope you find what you're looking for." Evie turned and walked off then, leaving Hannah shell-shocked and shaking. She'd left the party early. Claimed a work emergency and took an early flight back to San Francisco. And she'd cried the entire flight back.

Hannah pushed the memory aside before it reared full force. She had matters to discuss. Important matters.

"Why would Dad hire Danny Fletcher to renovate the kitchen?" Her heart sped up just mentioning his name.

Evie gave her a long look and then said, "Dan took over his father's contractor business. I thought you knew that."

She did. Of course she did. Even if she hadn't wanted to know. What Danny did with his life was his business. Just like what she did was hers.

"And there wasn't a single other contractor that Dad could have hired instead?"

Evie shrugged. "Dan's the best." She tipped her head, giving Hannah a look of such sympathy that for a moment, Hannah thought she could feed into it. "I know it was hard for you, what happened…"

"Please," Hannah scoffed, composing herself quickly. "That was years ago. A childhood romance. I've had plenty of boyfriends since Danny. More serious ones, too." Not true. A few dates. A few flings. But nothing serious. By choice.

"If you say so." Evie didn't look convinced.

"Why would you say that?" Hannah asked.

"Because you still call him Danny." Evie raised an eyebrow.

Well, she had her there. Years had passed. Danny had become Dan. A man. A father.

And she…she had nothing. A damaged relationship with her father. A worse one with her sister. No mother. No job. Her head began to spin.

Well. No need to worry about her current circumstances at the moment. There must be plenty of opportunities for a photographer in town. She was photographing Bridget's wedding. That was a start.

"Some habits are hard to break," was all she said. She jutted her chin at the bar behind Evie. "So you're going to be working here now?" It hardly fit into Evie's long-term plans. What about the grade-point average and the late nights studying?

"Just until I find something permanent," Evie said, looking away.

Well, that made two of them in transition then. Stuck back at home, in their childhood bedrooms, in twin beds. Evie's room was ballet pink; Hannah's was light blue. But the only difference separating them was that Evie didn't have her ex-boyfriend one floor below.

Right. Time to get on with the day. Talk to some people about work opportunities. Maybe get rich quick over night so she could get back on her feet. And out of Oyster Bay.

But the thought saddened her. Last time she had left, she had run to something. Now leaving again felt like running away.

"Well, I'll see you back at the house," she said as she slid off the stool. She could hear her dad's laughter through the swing door to the kitchen when a waitress burst out, carrying a tray of iced teas. Her heart panged, and she glanced at Evie, who was still watching her a little too closely.

"If you wanted to talk to Dad, he's probably just going over the inventory for tonight."

Hannah considered it, but now wasn't the time. She owed her father a talk, about a hell of a lot more than why he'd hired Danny of all people to renovate his kitchen, but she needed to do it when no one was around, her sister included.

"I have to get some stuff done," Hannah said, trying her best to ignore the look of judgment in Evie's face. It was subtle, but it was there. The pursed mouth, the slight lift of her left eyebrow. Evie was disappointed in her. And she was disappointed in herself.

She opened her mouth to say something, to explain, to

justify her choices, and then stopped. Another burst of tourists were coming through the door, and Evie was now trying to stave the panic off her face when one asked for a Bloody Mary.

Nope. Now was definitely not the right time for a heart to heart.

She wasn't sure when was. Sometimes, it was easier to just keep dodging the hard stuff than face it head on.

Chapter Four

Dan pulled his truck to a stop outside the old Cape Cod he'd lived in since he was a kid, only now it was no longer his parents' house, it was his, not that he'd changed it much. It had been a gift from his parents when he'd gotten married, a way to help them get settled. Alicia had never liked the house, though. Liked it even less than she'd liked him. He'd suggested they move, offered up repairs, worked on the bathrooms and the kitchen and even added a sun porch in his free time, but nothing helped. They'd married for all the wrong reasons. And all the right ones, too.

He sighed, feeling the weight of the day roll off his shoulders as he stepped out onto the gravel driveway. The sun was low in the horizon, blinding his view of the road, and for some reason he stared at it, daring for a moment to look back on a time in his life when he'd made a decision and stuck to it, daring for once to think of what he'd lost instead of what he had gained.

Enough of that.

He turned, walked into the house through the side door into the kitchen, where Mrs. Quinn was standing at the island, tossing a salad, and Lucy was at the table near the window, drawing in her sketchpad. When she heard the door slam shut, she looked up, a smile taking over her face that made his heart seize up every time like it was the first time. "Hi, Dad!"

Aw, see, so it wasn't so bad. She was the same little girl who would squeal with delight when he'd toss her into the waves, the same little girl who begged him to help her build a sandcastle, the same little girl who needed tucked in every night.

And that alone made every other painful day worth it.

"Hey, sweetheart." He walked over and dropped a kiss on the top of her head. "What are you drawing?"

Mermaids, it would seem. He idly wondered if she still believed in them and then decided not to ask. He'd rather keep on believing too.

"How was your day?" Mrs. Quinn asked, just as she always did. She was a part of their family in many ways, a daily fixture that he had come to rely on, especially in the past year and a half. With his own parents down in Florida and Alicia's parents in Portland, Mrs. Quinn filled the role of grandmother for Lucy, and lately, maybe even mother too. She took her to school on the days Dan had an early start, and in the summer, camp too. She cooked their dinners on the nights he worked late, and packed lunches, his included. Her daughter ran a day spa in town, and every few weeks she treated Lucy to a "Girls Day" where they got their nails painted. Lucy always came home with a smile on her face.

But it wasn't just Lucy who appreciated having Mrs. Quinn around. Dan did too.

"Not bad," he said, deciding to omit the part about running into Hannah, not that she would know the significance that played in his life. To most people in town, Hannah was a blip in his history. When they thought of him, they thought of Alicia, and how she'd left him. And Lucy.

"Met a good woman yet?"

Dan picked up the stack of mail and sifted through it. "Why is my romantic life so important to everyone in this town?"

"Because you don't have a romantic life," Mrs. Quinn said pointedly. "And you need a good woman, and she needs a mother." Mrs. Quinn had the decency to have whispered that last part, but Dan still glanced worriedly in his daughter's direction.

"We're doing just fine," he replied tersely, but the truth of that matter was that he worried every day that he wasn't enough.

"I know a nice girl you can take to this wedding," Mrs. Quinn was saying. Catching the confusion in his face, she tapped on the invitation to Bridget Harper's wedding that was attached to the fridge by a heart-shaped magnet Lucy had made when she was in preschool.

"It's too late to reply with a plus one," he said happily. Wonderful excuse. He really didn't need Mrs. Quinn talking up her single daughter anymore. Sure, Amanda was easy on the eye, but Dan had made it clear that he didn't need any more complications in his life, and dating Mrs. Quinn's daughter would be a complication.

Hell, dating anyone would be a complication.

"No problem," Mrs. Quinn said as she rinsed some cherry tomatoes in a colander. "She's invited too. Nice girl. Estelle's niece. Maybe you'll be seated together at the singles table."

"Mrs. Quinn…" he warned.

"Well, if you're not interested in her, then how about taking my Amanda? She's still single, and awfully pretty with that blonde hair…and I'm sure she'd love to go this wedding, even if it might be a little strange to see Zach Dillon back together with Abby Harper instead of her." Mrs. Quinn stared out the window for a moment and then sighed.

"I'm fine going on my own," he said firmly. He gave Mrs. Quinn a look that said he hoped that the conversation was now over, and after a long look of overt disappointment, she shrugged her shoulders and untied her apron strings.

"I'm off then," she said.

"You don't want to stay for dinner?" he asked casually,

hoping he hadn't offended her. At least half the time she did stay, especially since her husband had been gone for five long years after a short but intense battle with cancer, and he knew she enjoyed the company just as much as he did.

"Dan, if you are looking for female companionship, I am happy to give you a list of names. But I can assure you that mine will not be on it." She winked and patted his shoulder as she gathered up her bag and keys and said good-bye to Lucy.

"She's got a point, Dad," Lucy said, looking up from her sketch book. "Even I have a boyfriend."

Dan opened his mouth but nothing came out. Well, maybe a squeak.

He'd just be happy that she'd shared that with him. And as a single dad, he'd just have to learn to talk about these things. Somehow.

*

Hannah waited to go home until the sun was setting. The upside was that she'd gotten a few great shots of the tide coming in. The downside was that her stomach was rumbling and her feet were tired from walking. Even though she was sure that Dan would be long gone by now, she hovered at the edge of her father's driveway, behind an overgrown hydrangea bush in desperate need of pruning, and looked for any hint of the man in the house.

The lights in the kitchen were out. This and the fact that the truck wasn't in the driveway were two good signs.

With a sigh of relief, she walked up the gravel drive to the house, taking the front door, just in case.

"Dad?" But of course he wasn't home. He was probably at The Lantern, just as he had been every evening for as long as she could remember. She'd resented the restaurant when she was younger, blamed it for the reason her mother had left, said he cared more about working than his family. But now she knew it wasn't that simple. And she felt ashamed for ever thinking it was.

Her father was a hard-working man. And everything he had ever done was in an attempt to provide for his daughters. The fact that he'd waited this long to renovate his kitchen was proof of that.

The downstairs of the house was dark and silent, and Hannah toed off her flip-flops before creeping to the back of the house. The kitchen was empty, and Dan had clearly been busy. The cabinets had been stripped of their doors and half the shelving was gone, too. She opened the fridge, relieved to find that it was still plugged in, and better yet, filled with leftovers from the restaurant, the very same fare they'd lived on for nearly all of their childhood, with the exception of take-out pizza.

She opened a container and sniffed it. Lobster mac and cheese. She'd take it. She looked around to make sure the microwave was still in place, and quickly heated her dinner and grabbed a fork, eager to get out of the kitchen, away from any reminder of the man who had spent the day inside it. Inside her house.

It was wrong. Wrong, wrong, wrong.

She hurried up the stairs, noticing the glow under the closed door of Evie's bedroom, and, hesitating, crossed the landing to her own door. The room was the same as she'd left it when she was eighteen. A blue bedspread covered the white iron frame and the striped curtains still skimmed the worn floorboards.

She sank onto the window seat and took a bite of her food, closing her eyes at the taste. Straight off the kids' menu, it was her favorite meal growing up. Her dad used a special blend of cheddar and gouda and he promised to teach her the recipe someday. But like so many things in life, by the time she was old enough to ask for it, she'd lost interest.

She'd have to talk to her Dad. And soon. Put aside the stilted conversations that had become the norm, explain to him why she had to go, why she needed to be with her mother. She'd needed to know. It was a hole in her chest that was with her every day, and no amount of love and support could fill it. Only one person could fill it. The very same person who had put it there in the first place.

Hannah took another bite of her food, considering the irony of it all. All these years later and instead of the hole closing, it had grown bigger.

"Hey."

Hannah looked up to see Evie standing in the hallway,

wearing sweats and a college tee shirt. Her hair was pulled back in a ponytail and she was wearing her glasses, hiding her pretty blue eyes. Clearly in for the night, not that Hannah couldn't say the same. Tomorrow she might look up one of her friends from growing up, but tonight she didn't have the energy for it. She felt drained, and sad, and more confused than ever.

"Think Dad has any wine left, or did he clear it all out for the construction?" she asked.

Evie looked momentarily startled but a light started to gleam in her eye. "I'll go check."

A moment later they were climbing out of the upstairs bathroom window and onto the roof above the kitchen, Hannah finding she wasn't quite as nimble as she'd been back when she was a teenager, and Evie shaking so hard Hannah was more than a little concerned that her sister might just slide all the way down the gutter to the grass below.

The wine was cold, a screw top luckily, and Hannah let Evie take the first sip. "Why didn't we ever do this before?" she wondered aloud, as she looked out onto the sky and the stars above. She'd forgotten how clear the sky was in Oyster Bay. How you could find the Big Dipper and the Little Dipper. And her special star. The one her father had given to her. She squinted against the bright light of the moon, then slowly shifted her eyes to the right. Yep. There it was, Hannah's Star. Evie had one, too, but she couldn't remember where it was now.

"Because you were gone by the time we were old

enough to drink," Evie pointed out.

Oh that. True. But then the same could be said for Evie, only Evie's reason for staying away was possibly a little more acceptable, or at least, not quite so controversial.

"You never told me how it was," Evie said slowly. "Being with Mom."

Hannah took a long pull on the wine bottle, buying time. She wasn't sure what her sister wanted to know, or what she should even tell. Evie didn't remember their mother, who was gone before she was two. She had never experienced the same sense of loss or urge to connect with her. She was perfectly content with their dad and their Aunt Anne and their three cousins.

But Hannah remembered what it was like when her mother was still under this roof, even if the images were blurry and faded, maybe even distorted. She remembered the smell of her mother's perfume on the rare occasions that she and Chip went out on a date, leaving them with the neighbor's teenage daughter, who paid them no attention and watched MTV while she ate all their snacks and didn't share. She remembered other random things, like the way their mother dressed them in matching outfits for Christmas, and how she always had a novel on her bedside table, even if it was always the same one. And she remembered the arguments, that seemed to grow louder by the day, and the look on her father's face when he sat her down and explained that Mommy had gone away, and he wasn't sure when she was coming back.

Of course, she'd never come back, and somehow Hannah was still struggling to accept this, long after she'd stopped looking out the window for a hint of her mother's blue Dodge sedan with the cloth seats, the very one she'd thrown up in after a late night at Summer Fest with too many treats, or feeling the hope in her chest when she opened the door after school, wondering if this were the day she'd find her mother in the kitchen.

Instead she'd had to go after her mother herself, all the way to California, just to find her.

"You know about Kelly," she said carefully to Evie, and Evie nodded.

Kelly was only two years younger than Evie. The daughter that had been worth sticking around for, it seemed. Or, maybe, the daughter worth leaving them for.

It wasn't right. Or fair. But then, whoever said that life was fair? If life had been fair then their mother would have stuck around for them, too. Or visited or called. Or made them stop wondering why she couldn't love them, or if she even missed them. If life had been fair then she and Dan wouldn't have ever broken up and gone their separate ways. But life wasn't fair. And she knew that now.

"She's...nice. I like her," she admitted, even though it scared her to do so. She hadn't wanted to like Kelly, the girl who'd taken their mother, stolen her place. She had felt jealous of her, but fascinated too. But once she got to know her, she liked her, and she knew that it wasn't

Kelly's fault that their mother was sticking around for her when she couldn't be there for Hannah or Evie. It was luck of birth order, maybe, or just bad timing.

"That's okay," Evie said, giving her a small smile. "It's weird to me that I have a sister out there that I've never even met. It's taken a long time for me to get to used to it."

"You'd like her," Hannah said, knowing it was the truth.

Evie was thoughtful for a moment. "Maybe someday I'll have it in me to reach out to her, but for now...I'm good. I have everything and everyone I need right here in Oyster Bay."

Hannah knew it was true, and she envied her sister for that peace. "Mom was a giant disappointment," she blurted, hating the hurt that crept into her tone. The backs of her eyes prickled at the admission, and she took another swig of the wine, wishing it was a cure-all but knowing that it wasn't. She wanted to tell Evie every awful detail, but she was ashamed. Ashamed that she'd clung to hope that wasn't there. Afraid that Evie wouldn't understand why she had. Their mother drank. And she stayed out. And she had a mean streak. She wasn't like Aunt Anne, who had rosy cheeks and was always there for a hug. She was...hard. Once, when she'd worked up the courage, she asked Kelly if she'd always been like that, and Kelly grew quiet for a long moment, before admitting that she hadn't. But it would seem that her life in

California, like her life in Maine, was disappointing, so the happiness faded and the bitterness crept in. There were times, moments that were all too fleeting, when Hannah saw something in her mother, something that Chip must have seen. A sense of humor. A wit. An attraction. A pull. The woman's laugh was contagious. But just as quickly as she'd pull you in, make you feel drawn into a special, secret circle, she would let you go. And the times that Hannah sat and talked to her mom, dared to think that they were making progress, had only proven to her that they hadn't. Wouldn't. Couldn't.

"I shouldn't have gone out there. Shouldn't have tried. It was stupid of me."

"Don't beat yourself up about it," Evie said firmly. She held her eyes for a moment, until Hannah was convinced. "I was upset at first. I felt, well, betrayed, I guess. But I understand now. I guess I just didn't understand why you stayed out there so long. Why you stayed away."

"I came back for visits." Short ones. Ones where she stayed at the house as much as possible instead of venturing into town. And granted, it had been a few years, and the last visit hadn't gone well. She eyed Evie to see if she was thinking about that time, too. "And you were away at school."

"Yes, but…"

Hannah knew where this was going. She hadn't just gone away. She'd pulled away. But not because she didn't love her father or sister or even her life here in this house. But because she had to. She had to try and forge something with her mother, and she didn't know what else to do other than to hand herself over, because if she stayed here, in her heart, she would never be able to forgive the woman for what she'd done to their family.

And in the end, she still couldn't.

"Mom's having an affair," she said, taking another sip of wine. "Not her first." Kelly knew all about it. Had overheard some phone conversations and put two and two together. When she'd told Hannah, all Hannah could do was laugh. She knew it wasn't the compassionate response, but it was a validating one. Her mother couldn't be changed. She would always be out for herself, not caring who she hurt in her path.

Someday, if she dug deep enough, maybe Evie could analyze the reasons behind this behavior. Or maybe there was no reason. Maybe her mother just was who she was. Maybe it was time that Hannah accepted that.

"Was she like this when Dad was married to her?" Evie looked puzzled.

"Eventually," Hannah said with a sigh, recalling some conversations she'd had with Aunt Anne as she grew older. "But he loved her. And for a while, I'd like to believe that she loved him, too."

"I wonder if she ever loved us," Evie said, and all once she seemed like the younger sister again, not the wise, educated, insightful sibling.

Hannah thought of the way her mother had interacted with her all these years, tolerating her at arms' reach, never letting her in, never really trying. The distance was always there, even if it wasn't measured in mileage. "I wish I could say that she did, but I think the only person she really loves is herself." Hannah's chest felt heavy with regret. For hope that was lost. For time that was misspent. For dreams that hadn't come true.

"Well, I'm feeling sorry for myself."

"Hey, I asked." Evie held out her hand for the bottle. "Did you used to come out here before?"

Hannah laughed. "Of course. How else do you think I snuck off to see Danny?"

Evie chewed her lip. "You do know he's single again."

Hannah frowned at Evie, hating the way her heart started to speed up. "No," she said, hoping her voice sounded more neutral than she felt. "I didn't know that." How could she?

"His wife left him. Over a year ago. No one has seen or heard from her since."

"Sounds familiar," Hannah said bitterly, but she felt sad, in a way she didn't think she could feel sad for Dan, even if she would have expected to feel happy. The woman that had taken the only man she'd ever loved from her was now gone, out of the picture.

But what did that change? Nothing. Too much had happened.

"Well, it doesn't matter. That was a long time ago," she said, trying to convince herself even though she knew she wasn't convincing Evie. You couldn't put anything past her younger sister. She was sharp. And intuitive. And she was usually right, as annoying as that could be.

She stretched, started to stand, and inched back toward the window. "Heading in?"

"As if I'd let you leave me out here alone!" Evie's eyes were wide, and Hannah laughed.

She wasn't leaving Evie anywhere. She'd done it once. And it had cost her. And if spending time with her mother had taught her anything, in a roundabout way it had taught her just how important her family was to her.

Chapter Five

Hannah was up, showered, and out of the house by seven the next morning. She hadn't been active this early since her days at the magazine, and even then, it had required the use of two alarms and a whole lot of reluctance. She's always been that way. The last out of bed, barely making it to the school bus, with Evie standing there straight and ready, her lunch box in one hand, Hannah's in the other.

But today she was up long before the sun had risen and in town before the shops had turned their signs to OPEN. Today she wasn't taking any chances.

With her camera strapped around her neck, she stopped to snap a few shots of Main Street in its peaceful state, the warm morning light making her smile when she sat down at a bench to review her shots.

"Hannah Donovan!"

She looked up to see Beverly Wright approaching her with an overeager gleam in her eye. Hannah stifled a sigh. Mrs. Wright had always been a little too close for comfort, poking her head over the hedges the moment she heard the banging of the kitchen door, less than casually watchful as the girls played in the backyard or their dad grilled burgers. Hannah had never been sure what she was looking for. With her mother long gone, the fights had stopped, and Chip had never dated, never wanted to, so it wasn't like there was a revolving door of women or potential Mrs. Donovans to spy on. Still, Mrs. Wright persisted. Old habits die hard, Hannah supposed.

"Hello, Mrs. Wright," she said, smiling weakly. She supposed she was now old enough to refer to the woman as Bev, as others called her, but the Donovans and Wrights had never been close, and then, of course, there was the issue with Bev's pesky son...

"I heard you were back in town! For Bridget's wedding?"

For more than that, not that Hannah would be letting on. Luckily, Bev didn't wait for a response.

"Of course it's so nice to see the Harper girls all settling down, even if it did take a couple tries for Margo and Bridget." She gave a laugh, and Hannah braced herself for the inevitable. "How about you? Anyone special in your life?" She blinked a few times and then blatantly stared at Hannah, showing no signs of moving on, or even changing topic.

"Oh…" Hannah looked down the street just in time to see the light above Angie's come on. Of course the café would be open this early, and she could park herself there until she figured out what to do with her day. Or her life.

"No one at the moment," she replied, looking up to see the light that now shone in Bev's eyes. "I've been travelling."

"But now you're back!" Bev insisted. "And a girl as pretty as you shouldn't be single. At your age!"

Hannah frowned. She wasn't even thirty yet. Was that really such a travesty? Although considering that Bev had probably married at age twenty-two, and finished having all four of her children by age thirty, she supposed it was.

"Well," Bev said, a light filling her eyes. "I am sure my Timmy would just love to know that you are back in town and looking for an eligible bachelor!"

"I'm not looking…" Hannah didn't know why she had bothered. Bev was already pulling a scrap of paper from her handbag, a grocery store receipt that must have been at least two feet long, and scribbling something on it.

"You remember my Timmy, don't you?" Bev looked alarmed for a brief second before a warm smile took over her face. "Oh, but then who could forget my Timmy?"

Indeed, who could forget Timmy, who on more than one occasion had snuck into the girls' bathroom at school to have a peek under the stalls? And even though Timmy had eventually outgrown that devilish behavior, by the time he got to high school he had earned the unfortunate reputation of "Mama's Boy." Perhaps it was because he always had to call Bev to check in, or perhaps it was because Bev came to every track meet with her homemade banner and shouted, wolf-whistled, and cat-called when Timmy cleared a hurdle, or perhaps it was because Bev had Timmy take his younger sister to prom, even bought her a corsage, and when asked about it, he said his mother had made him do it. Tim wasn't so bad, really. A little hunched in the shoulders. A little nasal in the voice. A little creepy with the way he would hover in the halls and stare at the girls until they caught his eye and he would look away, face flaming to a shade of red that nearly matched his hair.

Hannah had no choice but to take the long curl of paper that was being thrust at her. She frowned at it. "Did you mean Mr. Wright?" she asked, pointing to the word that distinctly spelled "Mr. Right."

Bev just patted her shoulder and gave her a little wink. "I meant it exactly as I wrote it."

Hannah had been afraid of that. "Well. Thanks." She felt uneasy, not wanting to throw out the paper but not wanting to give false hope and hold onto it either.

She dropped her hand to her side, feeling the paper skim the side of her bare thigh. "Well, it was nice running into you, Mrs. Wright. I'm sure I'll see you around the house soon. I should probably go now, though. Time for my caffeine fix." She gave a forced smile, hoping for an easy exit.

"I must run, too. Off to see Linda McKinney's

daughter. You remember her? She's pregnant again. Number two! A girl!" She frowned at Hannah's flat stomach. "You'd better hurry up and get going on that before things stop working down there."

Hannah felt her jaw slack as Bev walked away, still rambling something about Timmy as she did.

She closed her eyes, counted to three, reminded herself that she had nowhere else to go, unless she wanted to try running back to California for a bit, and she had no interest in doing that ever again. Lesson learned. The hard way, of course. Wasn't that the only way?

With a long sigh that she hoped would give her some determination but instead only made her heart feel even heavier, she walked the block and a half to Angie's and ordered a coffee and a blueberry muffin and settled herself at a table in the far corner of the room with her back to the counter, where she hoped to be left alone until, well…forever?

She was just biting into her muffin when she saw a set of jean-clad legs appear in her periphery, and before she knew what was happening, the chair across from her was being scraped against the floorboards.

Dan dropped into it, giving her a sheepish smile across the table that made her pulse skip and her stomach do something fluttery and unwanted.

She glared at him.

So much for thinking this was her safe spot. She might as well have slept in, come downstairs at a leisurely hour, and dealt with him in the comfort of her own kitchen.

"What are you doing here?" she asked.

"Getting coffee." He checked his watch, giving her a look of confusion. "You're up early."

"Still on California time," she replied curtly.

His mouth twitched as his eyes narrowed. "But California is three hours behind us."

Oh. Right. "Well, I couldn't sleep," she said, her cheeks growing hot. She picked up her muffin and then thought better of it. Crumbs scattered on the plate.

Dan took a swig of his coffee. It was in a paper cup, but for some reason he seemed hell-bent on staying put.

"Trouble on your mind? A certain...Mr. Right?" When she met his eye in alarm, he tapped on the crumbled receipt where Bev had scribbled Timmy's phone number.

She relaxed a little. "That was our next-door neighbor, Beverly Wright. She's trying to set me up with Timmy."

"Peepin' Tim?" Dan's eyes went round in alarm and Hannah laughed for good, a hard burst of joy straight from the gut. The kind of laugh only Dan could get out of her. It felt so good.

Quickly, she pulled herself together. There was no use getting caught up like this. Dan had gone his way and she'd gone hers.

Yet here they were. Together. Who'd have thunk it?

"Timmy's had a dry spell with women," Dan said politely. "Since seventh grade."

Hannah laughed again. "And I'm not the girl to break it." She sighed and tucked the receipt under her plate. "It seems that it's a crime to be single in this town."

His eyebrow cocked with just enough interest to make her regret saying anything. So Dan was divorced. He was probably dating again.

"Tell me about it," he surprised her by saying. "It's even worse when they think they have your best interest at heart."

"It's not in your best interest to be dating?" Oh, why had she asked? What did it matter?

"I have no intention of getting involved with anyone, romantically," he said, and for some reason, Hannah felt disappointed. "It's too…complicated."

A look passed through them. Complicated. That was one word for it.

"I heard what happened with Alicia. I'm sorry," she said, even though she wasn't sorry, not entirely. She was…confused. A part of her had wanted Dan to hurt as much as she'd hurt, but a part of her also knew that he was making the best of a difficult situation, and she wasn't going to be the one to stop him.

"It is what it is. Life has a way of throwing you curveballs." Dan managed a little smile and his eyes, when they met hers, were sad. He cleared his throat. "So, you're just in town for Bridget's wedding?"

Hannah was grateful for the shift in topic. "I'm taking the photos." She left it at that. No need to go into more detail. Dan wasn't a part of her life anymore, and she wasn't a part of his. There were things that had happened, years of events that the other didn't know about. Happy moments, sad moments. Once they'd shared everything. Now they were just two strangers, who had aged, and lived, and somehow ended up in the same café at the crack of dawn, probably each hoping to avoid the other.

"Your dad said you work at a magazine." Dan looked impressed, and for a moment, Hannah thought it would be easier to go along with it, pretend she still had the job. But she'd never been a good liar. Besides, Dan knew her too well. Even now, after all these years, she was sure she couldn't get one past him.

"I'm no longer at the magazine. I spent the past year travelling in South America. I'm hoping to put together a collection of photographs."

"For a book? Or a gallery?" Dan sipped his coffee and Hannah felt uneasy. He was making conversation, asking about her life, acting like there wasn't an unspoken history between them and hurt. So much hurt.

"A book maybe. I'm not really sure." She tucked a strand of hair behind her ear, that knot of anxiety forming in her gut again.

He nodded thoughtfully, as if piecing something together. "Well, if you're looking for opportunities in town, there's always the newspaper. And there's a studio down near the edge of town."

She blinked at him, surprised by his kindness as much as she knew she shouldn't be. They hadn't ended things badly. More like...sadly. And maybe this was his way of trying to make something up to her.

"Thanks," she said, managing a small smile. "I'll look into it." And she would. As soon as he left and she could gather her wits about her.

"So who are you going to the wedding with?" Dan asked.

"No one," she replied flatly.

He whistled under his breath. "It won't be that easy. And if you think you can get by sipping champagne and chatting with your girlfriends, you're sadly mistaken. Every busybody in town is invited to that wedding, and they're on a mission to set you up."

"Oh God, you're right," Hannah groaned.

"But, I have a solution," Dan said, grinning. He leaned back in his chair and looked at her, and for one long, horrible moment, Hannah allowed herself to look back. At the crinkly eyes that had fresh laugh lines at the corners, and the smile that curled ever so slightly at the corners. And the lips...that could perform magic.

"What's that?" she said, looking back at her coffee mug. It was half-empty, and probably cold by now, and she had lost all interest in finishing it. Still, she picked it up, as something to do. Something to...distract her.

"We can go together."

Hannah choked on her sip of coffee, happy that it was indeed cold and hadn't burned her mouth. "Go together?" She stared at him, her heart beginning to pound. Did he mean...? Was he implying...? "I don't follow."

"We give people something else to talk about. Or

something to silence them. Depends how you look at it."

"Wait." Hannah set down her mug, shaking her head. "You mean, we should go together? Like, together?"

"Like, on a date," Dan clarified, and just as Hannah's chest began to lift, he added, "A pretend date. We'll pretend we're dating, and that way everyone will leave us alone."

Pretend to be dating. Of course.

Hannah didn't know why the mere suggestion made her heart sink and the backs of her eyes prickle. Maybe it was because the last time she and Danny were together like this they were together for real. No pretending about it. She loved him and he…Well, he'd loved her once. But now. Now he was a father. He'd been married. Built an entire life with someone else. He'd had a family. And she was just some girl he once knew. A girl so detached from his world that he was comfortable just pretending to be dating her.

She wanted to say no. Hell no, to be exact, but what would be her reason? It was a good idea, as ridiculous as it was. And she really didn't need Bev pushing Timmy on her, or being asked to dance with every eligible man south of forty-five. But to spend the time with Dan? Pretending that her heart didn't break every time she looked into those eyes, or heard the rumble of his voice, or thought of what could have been and what hadn't been?

"What's the big deal?" Dan asked. "Unless you're uncomfortable spending time with me."

Her eyes flashed on him. As if she would give Danny Fletcher a reason to think he had moved on with his life but she hadn't moved on with hers!

"Please. What we had was ancient history. Kid stuff."

Something in his eyes wavered, but he said nothing.

"Fine. We'll go to the wedding together." Had she really just said that? The implication settled heavily on her. There would be dinner. And dancing. And laughter. And...him. She hadn't wanted to be near Dan since the horrible night when he'd told her about Alicia. About the baby. About one indiscretion that had taken place when they were on a silly break that would change every plan they'd ever put into place.

And now, she had just agreed to pretend that none of that mattered. That she hadn't cried herself to sleep for a year, that she hadn't imagined every step of his rapidly changing life, that she hadn't struggled to accept the permanency of it.

But now, Dan was single again. And so was she. And instead of being squished against Timmy all night long, she would suffer through a few hours of nostalgia.

After all, it was just one night. How much trouble could that be?

*

Evenings were always the worst time. Once Lucy was in bed, the house was too quiet. It allowed too much room for noise that wasn't welcome. Thoughts and worries that filled his head and didn't seem to go away, no matter how much he tried to busy himself with other things. Sometimes it was paperwork. Other times it was television. But it all came back to the same concerns. Would Lucy be okay? Had he done enough? What more could he have done?

He'd married Alicia. Committed to her. And the baby. And he'd fulfilled that promise. He'd given up his life in exchange for another, and he'd never allowed himself to look back.

Until this week.

Hannah. His sweet, happy Hannah. The girl who made him smile, the girl who'd grown up at his side. The girl he'd danced with at every school dance and laid with on the sandy shores, imagining their entire life stretched out ahead of them, as wide and open as the sea.

Dan walked to the fridge and pulled out a beer. Mrs. Quinn had made a taco salad tonight, and she'd saved what hadn't been eaten in plastic containers. He grabbed the box and took a fork from the drawer and went into the den to see if the game was still on.

Summer was almost over. In a few weeks, Lucy would be starting school. Another school year where her mother wouldn't be here to ask about her first day. He'd bring her out for ice cream, like he always did, to celebrate. Last year, out of nowhere, Lucy had burst into tears, asking where Alicia was, if she was coming back, and why she had left.

And Dan didn't have any answers. That was the worst

of it, feeling helpless, feeling confused and guilty and wishing he could turn back time.

But how far back, he wondered, thinking again of Hannah. She was still pretty. Still very much the same, really. He hadn't asked about her. It wouldn't have been appropriate. Even when Chip Donovan had called him over for the kitchen job, Dan had kept their interaction strictly professional. He'd always liked Chip. Still saw him every once in a while at The Lantern. He knew that Chip understood. Life could be strange. You did the best you could. He'd done the best he could.

He took another sip of his beer. Focused on the game and forked another bite of food into his mouth.

Had he done the best he could? When he thought of the little girl upstairs, asleep in the pale pink room, who was shutting down and shutting him out and hiding emotions that only sometimes came out, he wondered if he had.

He hadn't loved Alicia. But he'd loved Lucy. And he'd always love Lucy.

And Hannah. He'd always loved Hannah. And a part of him, he realized, with an uneasy feeling, still did.

Chapter Six

Evie wasn't sure exactly what it said about the current state of her life that, three days into the job, she had started to look forward to tending bar. When her father had given her a pass that morning, offered to let her take over the hostess stand for a bit this afternoon instead, she was nearly certain that the panic showed in her face.

Who would Ron have to talk to about his wife if she wasn't there refilling his glass? Jill was moving out yesterday, and Evie was eager to know if Ron had followed her advice about staying out on the boat until she was gone, or if he'd done what he said he wanted to do, which was to park himself on the couch and watch, and then tail her car, because he just knew that she was going straight to Dave's house and not to her sister Jessie's like she'd said.

In the end, Chip must have bought her excuses about needing to keep busy, and of course the tips that came with bartending didn't hurt either, she was sure to mention. After all, much as he loved her and was happy to have her back in town, she was also pretty sure he didn't want her living with him forever. He definitely hadn't been happy to pound on the upstairs bathroom door for a solid five minutes this morning, waiting for Hannah to finish showering, and when her sister had emerged, cheeks flushed and hair perfectly coiffed, Evie and Chip could only look at each other in confusion. Since when did Hannah rise so early? Back in high school, Evie would have to flick her lights and Chip would have to threaten to make her walk to school in the snow.

But then, of course, Dan Fletcher was working on the kitchen, and even though Hannah seemed to leave every morning before he arrived, no doubt she was primped and ready, just in case they had a run-in.

Evie mixed a margarita for the two girls who were perched at the end of the bar, thinking that she was really starting to get the hang of this. Most folks had simple orders: beer, wine, Long Island iced tea. This was a casual restaurant with fading nautical decorations and a deck with panoramic views, not exactly a trendy establishment like her cousin Bridget's ex-husband's place. Dunley's had live music and it was what Ryan had always insisted be called a "gastro pub," a term that made Chip roll his eyes when he thought no one was looking, but Evie never missed much.

She checked her watch. It was nearly five and Ron hadn't stopped in yet. Concerning. If he wasn't back by tomorrow, she'd call on her cousin Margo's husband Eddie, the sheriff, to see if poor Ron had gone against her better advice and done something stupid.

"Hey, Evie!"

Evie turned around to see her sister sitting at the counter, her camera strapped around her neck, her cheeks a little pinker than usual. She grinned back at her sister, a little hesitantly. Sure, it had been fun the other night, sharing a bottle of wine, talking like sisters should, like her Harper cousins did. But it didn't erase the hurt that had lingered in her chest for years, long after Hannah had gone off to find their mother.

Hannah liked their other sister. She actually knew her, had a relationship with her, understood her quirks and her qualities and everything that made her who she was. Everything that made her the daughter their mother was willing to stick around for.

She could still remember when she'd first learned she even had another sister. The fascination had quickly been replaced with anger, and a pain so deep that she couldn't even hide it from her father. She'd broken her own rule, showing any sort of emotion about their mother in front of him. She knew he missed her. Even years after she was gone, any mention of her name and his eyes would cloud over, the way they now did when someone mentioned his sister Anne, who had died in that car accident, leaving

Bridget, Margo, and Abby without a mother…or a father.

See? You don't have it so bad, she'd told herself. No real reason to complain. She still had a father, and her poor cousins didn't.

But it didn't matter. It didn't replace the knowledge that the Harper sisters' parents had been taken from them, whereas Evie and Hannah's mother had chosen to leave. The Harper girls had years and years of happy memories to look back on. Christmases spent baking cookies and back to school shopping trips in Portland. They had a mother to turn to when stuff got weird, like with boys or school dances, or other things that Evie had no one to ask, even though Aunt Anne did offer.

They had time. And photos. And Evie had none of that to hold onto. Her mother was alive and well and living in California with her new family. And she didn't want to know a thing about it. The other night had been a slip. She'd gotten curious. And she'd been worried about Hannah. Professional habit and all that.

"What have you been up to today?" she asked her sister.

"Taking some photos," Hannah said, and Evie wondered how anyone could spend nearly eleven hours taking photos. But then, Hannah was always the type who lost track of time, only remembered to stumble home for dinner on summer nights when the sun was setting and her stomach was growling. And by then, Evie had chewed off all her fingernails, worried that Hannah had drowned at the beach, or tripped and hit her head on a rock, or some other disaster that would take her away too.

And then one day her worst fear did come true, didn't it? Hannah left.

"I'm heading over to see Bridget soon if you want to join me."

Evie hesitated. Her shift was ending, and she didn't have any other plans, unless worrying about her education going to waste counted as a good way to spend a summer evening.

"Why not?" she grinned, untying her apron as Chris came around the bar, a good-looking guy who made the girls with the margaritas nudge each other and giggle.

Evie stifled an eye roll. Really! So the man was attractive. He had a symmetrical face. Was that really so special? And nice hands, sure. And nice hair. And yes, a nice smile. But was that really worth making some fool of yourself for? She wanted to suggest to these girls that they spend their evening watching the science channel—or better yet, reading a book—instead of ogling at a bartender that would never remember their names the next morning. But she refrained. After all, no one liked unsolicited advice, even if she was happy to offer it!

"You look concerned," Hannah said as she hopped off the stool.

Images of Ron being cuffed and hauled off to the slammer filled her mind. He didn't like confined spaces. It was one of the arguments he gave for not wanting to take her advice and sleep on the boat for a few days. Claimed working the docks didn't make him a yachtsman.

He wouldn't do well in jail. Oh dear...

She glanced over to see Hannah watching her with a pinched brow. With a weak smile she said, "It's just one of my patients. I mean—" Jesus! Where did that come from? "I mean, one of my customers." She laughed uneasily.

"Here?" Hannah pushed through the door, frowning as if this was absurd, as it probably was.

"Well, he's a regular...he's been here every day this week." Evie shrugged. "His wife cheated on him."

"Ouch."

"Isn't that what happened with Dan?" Evie didn't want to sound like she was gossiping, but it had been big news in town at the time, and she'd heard from more than one busybody that he hadn't adjusted to life as a single father very well. And the man was in their house all day every day. She couldn't help but care.

"Beats me," Hannah shrugged. She licked her bottom lip, like she was just about to say something and then stopped herself. "Have you decided what you're going to wear to the wedding?"

It was only a few days away, and Evie hadn't give it any thought at all. It wasn't like her to procrastinate. She was more of a lists person. She had a list for everything, usually. What she would buy at the grocery store. What chores she would accomplish that weekend. What she needed to do to achieve her life plan. So much for that one.

"I'll probably just wear a black cocktail dress. It doesn't really matter."

"Hey, now," Hannah chided. "You never know if you'll meet a cute guy there."

Evie leveled her sister with a look. "I went to school with all of them just like you did, remember? Besides, I'm not in a place in my life to date."

"Me either," Hannah said quickly. "But, I sort of have a date."

"To the wedding?" Evie didn't know why her heart sort of sank at her sister's confession. "Who?"

"Danny," Hannah said, looking down at the ground.

"Danny? Dan Fletcher? The Dan I just asked you about? Your old boyfriend Dan?" Evie knew she sounded like the crows that used to wake her up in the morning, far too early, but she couldn't help it. Hannah had been dodging Dan all week. And now they were going as a couple to the wedding?

This didn't make sense. None of it. She was an expert in human behavior (regardless of what the people on that hospital board thought) and something wasn't adding up here.

"It's no big deal. He was going to be there, and I was going to be there, so...we'll go together."

No. Evie failed to believe it could be that simple. "Are you guys like...friends?"

Hannah looked shifty. "Not friends. Just...going to a wedding together."

It was clear that Hannah wasn't going to elaborate, and Evie wasn't going to pry. But it didn't mean it would stop her from getting to the bottom of this.

She hadn't grown up in a coastal town not to know when something smelled fishy, and this was very, very fishy indeed.

*

Hannah couldn't believe the improvements that Bridget had made to the big Victorian house the Harper girls had grown up in with their parents and grandmother. The rooms were light and airy with pastel-hued throw pillows and water colors on the walls, and even though it was now an inn and technically a business, it felt more like home than perhaps it ever had before.

"This is the ideal setting for your wedding," Hannah said, as she stepped out onto the back porch and breathed in the sweet salty air as she looked out onto the sea. It was just as peaceful now as it had been Monday morning, but there was always something special about the seaside at sundown, when the sky was filled with pastel colors.

"Margo was married here in the spring and it brought her luck, and this is where Jack and I met. It's my fresh start."

Hannah squeezed her cousin's hand. "I'm so happy for you."

And she was. Though she hadn't been there to witness Bridget's struggles firsthand, she knew what her cousin had been through, losing her parents shortly after having a baby, and then realizing her marriage was over not long afterward. She was strong, Bridget was, and this inn was proof of that.

"You've built an amazing life for yourself," she said, truly in awe. Really, could she have done the same for herself? When her life fell apart, she ran, first to South America and then here, because she had nowhere else to go. But then she supposed she had that luxury. Being single. Not being a mother.

She paused. Being a mother wasn't the excuse. Her own mother had run. Never looked back.

"It wasn't without a fair bit of risk," Bridget said, leading them over to a wicker table in the corner of the enclosed sun porch, where a pitcher of lemonade was waiting. If there were guests at the inn, Hannah wasn't aware, because the property was quiet and tranquil. Everything a country inn should be, she supposed.

"And you know it isn't like me to take risks," Bridget said with a laugh as she poured them all a glass.

Evie still looked a little rattled from the walk over. "No. It's not like any of us. Well, except for Hannah."

Hannah looked at her sister, detecting an edge to her tone. If she was implying that going out to California was a risk, she would have to disagree. It was foolish. But she was too tired to argue right now. Besides, why spoil the evening for Bridget?

"Abby," Hannah pointed out. "Abby is a risk taker."

"Yes, and no," Bridget said, looking thoughtful. "Abby bounced around a lot, never committing to anything for a while, but I actually think it's because she was avoiding risk. Taking a risk means, well, putting yourself on the line. Opening yourself to the possibility that things won't work out as you'd hoped."

So maybe Evie had been right. Again. She had taken a risk by going to California. She'd opened her heart up to rejection and hurt. And she wouldn't be making that mistake again.

"And Abby's catering the wedding?" Hannah asked.

"She insisted on it, but I want her to be my maid of honor, so she's agreed to make the cake. I thought you knew that your dad was catering the wedding. Well, his restaurant is catering it, I should say."

"I knew that." Evie gave Hannah a blank stare, and Hannah took a long sip of lemonade that she hoped would cool the heat from her cheeks.

"I must have forgotten," she said, even though it wasn't true. She and her father had barely said more than a few pleasantries to each other since she'd arrived in town. She knew he would be happy to say more, that it was she who was keeping the distance. She knew he'd smile and say something sweet and offer up anything she wanted. But there was a hurt in his eyes that would be there. A hurt that she couldn't bear to see just yet.

"And you're taking another risk," Evie said.

Hannah frowned at her sister and saw a defiance in her eyes that made her uneasy. "I don't know what you're talking about."

Evie jutted her chin and looked at their cousin. "Hannah and Dan are going to your wedding together."

Bridget's eyes widened and she stared at Hannah for a moment. "Is this true?"

"Yes and no," Hannah said. She glared at her sister. "Since we were both going to be there, we thought, we'd just go together."

"But what does this mean?" Bridget asked, leaning forward in her chair.

Evie tipped her head and narrowed her eyes on her. "Yes, Hannah. What does this mean?"

Hannah bit back a sigh of frustration. She should have known it wouldn't be so easy to pull this off. "It doesn't mean anything," she said firmly. And it didn't. It couldn't.

"Well," she said, desperate to change the subject. "Tell me all the details of how you and Jack met."

And so she sat and listened to how Jack had been a guest at the inn, and how, in the most unexpected of ways, a second chance had found Bridget.

"Listening to Bridget, it makes you almost believe there's hope for anyone," Evie said as they headed home.

Hannah nodded, thinking of her parents, of her mother, and most of all Dan. She'd come further with Dan than she'd ever imagined. Speaking to him. Even seeing him. And agreeing by some foolish act of defense to go with him to this wedding...

But a second chance? Maybe there was such a thing.

But even so, she wasn't putting her heart on the line to find out.

Chapter Seven

Dan was late. It was fine by Hannah, really, considering that she was running late herself. She'd slept in, leaving little chance of getting out the door without a run-in with her ex, unless she used the old bathroom window trick, and she didn't trust her legs at her age.

She put on a sundress, pulled her hair into a ponytail, and strapped her camera around her neck. She was meeting Bridget and Jack at ten to take some pre-wedding photographs of the happy couple, and she hoped to stop by the office of the *Oyster Bay Gazette* on the way and see if the newspaper had any need for a photographer.

She was almost to the last step on the stairs when she heard the back door swing shut and she knew, the way you just know, that it wasn't Evie or her father. It was Dan.

She eyed the front door greedily. She could slip out, dodge him for another day. But then she thought of their agreement—the one she really should cancel. She heaved a sigh. She would speak to Dan. She had to get used to it if she was staying in Oyster Bay for a while, after all. Maybe the more she did it, the easier it would become.

She almost burst out laughing. As if.

With nonchalance she certainly did not feel, she walked down the hall to the back of the house and hovered in the doorway to the kitchen long enough to enjoy the pull of Dan's tee shirt along his back as he pulled the last of the upper cabinets free from the wall.

He turned, suddenly noticing her, and she jumped a little. "Don't mind me," she said hurriedly. "I'm heading out. I just thought I'd grab something for breakfast on the way." There was a fruit bowl on the kitchen table, and half the contents of the pantry, too. She reached for a granola bar and an apple and stuffed both into her tote bag.

He motioned to the camera. "You always carry that thing with you?"

Pretty much, she thought, realizing how little he knew her anymore. Back when they were dating, photography had only been an interest. It wasn't until she was older that she started pursuing it more seriously. She never tired of the moments she could capture, forever frozen in time. Of the small glimpses of life that she could almost make sense of if she stared at the photograph long enough.

"I'm meeting Bridget and Jack for a photo session,"

she explained. "They wanted me to get a few shots of them together before the rehearsal dinner tomorrow night."

"Rehearsal dinner?" Dan cocked an eyebrow. "I wasn't invited to that."

"It's family only," Hannah explained, grateful for a quick excuse. "And a few friends in the wedding party."

A strange smile curved his mouth as he leaned back against the countertop and crossed his arms. "Shouldn't I be your plus one?"

She stared at him. He could not be serious. "I thought you said wedding date," she clarified. "And about that—"

"Well, if we're going to pull this off, we may as well be convincing." He shrugged. "Unless you want people to start setting you up again. Will Mr. Right be there tonight?"

If he was alluding to Timmy, then the answer would be no; however, that hadn't stopped her from darting her eyes to the hedge every time she entered or left the house. Dan was right—it would be a lot easier to just pretend they were a couple. Everyone would get off her back. She could live in peace. Go about her merry way.

Hannah pinched her mouth together. "Fine," she growled and grabbed another granola bar. It would be a long day in town avoiding him. "But no funny business."

She could have sworn she heard him chuckle as the screen door slammed shut behind her.

*

An hour later, and still not any happier at the thought of now having to spend two nights in a row with Danny, Hannah at least had one thing to celebrate. The *Gazette* had been in search of a photographer, just like Dan had mentioned, and they were happy to take her on. Her salary was a mere fraction of what she'd been earning at the magazine, but this was Oyster Bay, she told herself, and it would at least be something for her resume.

She'd thank Dan tomorrow. It wouldn't kill her. Lots had nearly killed her, but doing the right thing came with the territory.

The right thing. Those were the words Danny had used that awful night, when he'd sat her down and told her that he was marrying Alicia. That she was expecting his baby and that he had proposed. She'd almost laughed out loud at first. After all, he wasn't even nineteen yet! How could he get married? And how could he ever get married to anyone other than her?

It had happened because they'd had a fight. Two weeks of silence over an argument about Hannah's desire to go out to California, and Dan not supporting it. Why go chasing after a new life when you have everything you ever wanted right here? That was his rationale. It was the unanimous rationale. But he didn't understand. No one did. Not even Evie. Or Aunt Anne. She had a mother out there. And she had to connect with her. Or at least try.

She'd applied to colleges exclusively on the West Coast for this reason, and Dan had done the same, but he'd applied to a few others, she'd learned. University of Maine, for example. UMass, too. When she'd discovered this, she felt betrayed, and hurt, and he'd reminded her again that everything they loved was right here in Oyster Bay, including each other.

She'd burst into tears, telling him he didn't know her at all then, and didn't speak to him for two weeks. By the time they were back together, he'd admitted that he'd been upset one night, had too many of his dad's beers, went to a party down at the beach with Doug McKinney and some of the girls on the cheerleading squad. Alicia was nice to him. Tried lifting his spirits. And things had happened. He didn't mean it. He was sorry. The only girl he really loved was her.

And what could she say? He hadn't cheated, not really. They'd been on a break. And he loved her. And she loved him. And it had been their first fight. So they kissed and made up and when she saw Alicia in the halls at school, she knew that it didn't matter. Danny was back with her. He was putting the West Coast schools at the top of his list, and with any luck, in September, they'd be off to Los Angeles or San Francisco to start their life together.

But they didn't end up in California together. They didn't end up anywhere together. A month later Dan sat her down, told her that he wasn't going to college at all. He was going to start working at his dad's contracting business. He was going to be a father. He was getting married.

He was doing the right thing. And that's what he'd done.

And what had Hannah done?

All the wrong things, she thought, as she dropped onto a bench outside Town Hall, where she'd agreed to meet Bridget and Jack, who were picking up their marriage licenses this morning.

She decided to take a few shots of them in town. The gazebo in the town green would be a beautiful backdrop, and the pier was a pretty location too. She had time, and she knew that Bridget had cleared the inn starting this morning, even directing wedding guests to the Oyster Bay Hotel so she didn't feel "on duty" for her big weekend.

A tap on her shoulder made her jump. She looked over her shoulder to see Bev Wright peering down at her, a satisfied smirk on her face and Timmy firmly at her side.

Well, crap. It seemed that even if she could dodge certain people on her own property, Oyster Bay was far too small to be spared indefinitely.

"Hello, Mrs. Wright," she said pleasantly. "Hello, Timmy." She'd barely seen him on her last visit, only in passing on the driveway and through the hedge, but he hadn't changed much from the freckle-faced schoolboy he'd been back in school.

"It's Tim," he grunted, his brow pinching.

"Tim." Of course. Only his mother called him Timmy. And really, wasn't he technically Mr. Right? She had to press her lips together to keep from laughing out loud at that.

Poor Tim had been trussed up in a suit and tie, no doubt on parade for an eligible wife, given that he worked at his father's pharmacy, as he had since high school. Hannah watched the Adam's apple roll in his throat and had the dreaded feeling that he was going to put them all in an awkward position soon.

"Timmy?" Bev elbowed Tim so hard that he nearly lost his footing. "Don't you have something you wanted to ask Hannah?" She darted her eyes so obviously toward Hannah and back again, that Hannah was almost alarmed at the thirty seconds of silence that it took for Tim to catch on.

Finally, he cleared his throat.

Hannah closed her eyes.

"Hannah," he said stiffly.

When he didn't say anything more, against her far better judgment, she said, through gritted teeth, "Yes?"

"Will you...do me the honor...of...going as my date..."

"To the wedding!" Bev finished for him, her voice shrill. "To Bridget's wedding! Timmy was invited, of course. We all were!"

Hannah gave an apologetic smile and took a deep breath. "I'm sorry, Tim, but I already have a date."

"You have a date?" Bev accused sharply. Her eyes were so wide that Hannah could see the whites all around them.

"Dan and I are going together." She knew that

delivering that line shouldn't have felt has good as it had. They were not back together. They couldn't be. Their time had come and gone. And she'd accepted that.

And now…now her pulse raced at the mere mention of the man's name, and her stomach did this fluttery thing, and her mind actually dared to come up with a million excuses for how this time it could be different. Dan wasn't married anymore.

But Dan had been married. He had married someone else. Broken up with her. Broken her heart. And she'd be best to remember that. After all, where had following her heart gotten her yet?

"Dan Fletcher?" Bev's eyes flashed. "Well, I see. Yes, I *see*!"

"We used to date," she pointed out, as if this piece of Oyster Bay history were ever truly forgotten. "Before…"

She trailed off. Everyone no doubt knew what that meant. Before Dan and Alicia. Before Lucy. She remembered scanning the birth announcements, wanting to know the name and gender of Dan's child almost as much as she longed not to think of it. But this baby was a part of Dan, and she loved him, and so she couldn't let it go. And she'd finally found it one day, sitting at a computer station in the school library. A girl. Lucy. Lucy Fletcher. A baby weighing seven pounds, six ounces. A small, tiny human being that had set big events into emotion.

She'd left the library, hiding her tears until she was back in her dorm room. And she'd cried all night, thinking of Dan with Alicia. And now Dan with Alicia and Lucy. And how he probably never even thought of her any more, and that really, he shouldn't. And that she shouldn't think of him either. It was over. The baby made it permanent.

Only now…Now Alicia was gone. Now it was just Dan and Lucy.

"Well!" Bev sniffed. She jerked her arm through Tim's elbow. "Come along, Timmy. We have important business to attend to at the pharmacy, don't we?"

Bev hurried away, no doubt to tell all her friends about how Hannah and Dan were together again, and Hannah could only sigh as she watched her go.

No going back now.

*

At six o'clock the next evening, Dan emerged, showered and dressed, into the kitchen of his childhood home, where he'd lived all his life, first as a child and then as a young husband and now, as a single father.

And never in his entire thirty years stepping into this kitchen had he felt so uncomfortable.

Mrs. Quinn stared. Lucy's eyes popped. "Did somebody die, Dad?" she asked fearfully.

"What?" He looked at his daughter in confusion. "Of course not. Why would you ask that?"

"You're wearing a tie," she said, pointing at him. "I've never seen you wear a tie."

He looked down at the light blue tie he had pressed against his white dress shirt. His neck felt tight and he longed to loosen the damn thing, but he refrained. "People wear ties for all sorts of reasons, honey," he assured her.

"Name one!" She looked at him in challenge, and Dan bit back a sigh. She was becoming stubborn, giving him a run for it half the time, but the other half of the time she was still sweet, still happy to curl up on the couch and watch a movie with him. Until her friends started calling, of course. Or she grew silent, and sullen, no doubt thinking of her mother.

"I can think of a reason." Mrs. Quinn said, barely suppressing a smile as she set the bowl of pasta on the table and doled out two plates, one for her, and one for Lucy.

"I'm going to Bridget and Jack's rehearsal dinner," Dan reminded her. It was the excuse he'd given for asking her to stay late this evening, and he was sticking to it.

He hesitated. Wasn't the reason for this plan to get insinuations like this to stop? But that would mean leading Lucy to believe that there was someone in his life. And there wasn't.

"I won't be out late," he said, as he opened the back door.

"Don't hurry back! Take your time! Enjoy!" Mrs. Quinn called after him, even as he was quickly starting the engine to his truck.

He turned up the music and rolled down the windows, enjoying the sea breeze that blew out all the dust and sweat that seemed to fill the vehicle from long days on the job. He was nervous, and why shouldn't he be?

The only girl he'd ever loved was back in town. And try as he might, he couldn't pretend that didn't get under his skin.

The rehearsal dinner was being held at the country club—an old institution at the northern edge of town. He felt out of place in his pick-up, especially when a white-gloved man came around and asked for his keys. Valet. Of course.

Dan reluctantly exited his vehicle and tugged at his tie. Music was filling the air, and he followed the sound of it, through the long hall, with a glance to his right where the dining tables were being set up, anchored by pink centerpieces, and through the French doors onto a wide veranda.

He hadn't even closed the door behind him when he saw her, standing on the edge of the lawn, her brown hair blowing in the breeze. Her laughter closed the distance between them, and she smiled that smile that went straight to his gut.

He smiled too. He couldn't help himself. He could have stood here and watched her talking to her cousins all night, but time was ticking by and he'd lost enough of it already.

With more determination than he felt, he took the

stairs down to the grass and walked over to Hannah, knowing it was time to play the part of happy couple.

The role came naturally, he realized. And he wasn't so sure that was a good thing.

Chapter Eight

Be still her heart. He was here. And he was wearing a suit and tie.

But then, of course he was. This was a formal affair. Still, a part of her couldn't help but feel that he'd dressed up for her.

Nonsense. The man had been married. He'd had a child with another woman. An entire life with another woman. Christmases and birthdays and lazy Sundays and a thousand memories that they alone shared and that she had never been a part of.

If there was any woman that Dan was missing these days, it was probably his wife.

The thought of it cut her, and she had to look away when he approached, his gaze cautious to her, but his smile bright as he gave greetings all around and congratulated Bridget and Jack.

She looked down at her dress, a light blue cotton dress that she'd had for years and rarely worn, smoothing it at the waist, grateful that her cousins were still at her side, but knowing that she couldn't cling to them all night. If they were going to pull this off, she had to look sincere.

Instead, she jumped when Dan suddenly slid a hand around her waist. She looked up at him with accusation in her eyes, she was sure of it, but he just cocked an eyebrow and turned back to Zach Dillon, Abby's boyfriend.

Once, her ex-boyfriend.

Still, Hannah wouldn't get caught up in that sort of fantasy. So Abby and Zach had found their way back together. Their break up had been a lot less complicated, as in, no one got married to someone else. No one had a kid with someone else. No one had their world completely turned upside down.

"So…" Abby dragged out the word as her eyebrows began to waggle. She grabbed Hannah by the elbow, rattled off an excuse of needing to get more champagne cocktails over her shoulder, and led them away from the men. "You and Dan are back together? Bridget told me you were going to be together at the wedding, and now tonight too?"

"Just each other's plus ones," Hannah said weakly. She knew she could confide in Abby. Abby would understand. They were friends that way. Kindred spirits really. Once, when they were little, she used to talk to

Abby about missing her mother, and Abby would offer to give her some of her dolls to take home to keep her company, because she probably didn't know what else to do. Without fail, the next day, she'd get an invite from Aunt Anne to do something "special" and Hannah would know that Abby had been behind it and she loved her for it, even if sometimes the days with Aunt Anne made her long for a mother of her own more than ever.

She looked down at her silver sandals as they climbed the stairs back into the clubhouse, trying to think of an excuse for why she was here with Dan, without giving anyone in her family false hope. "Both of us were tired of people trying to set us up, so we decided to come together."

Abby took this information in with a narrowing of her eyes. "But you're not really back together?"

"No." Oh, why did that statement have to hurt her heart so much? She knew where she stood, with Dan, with love in general. It didn't last. Not the romantic kind. Not even the other kind. There was no guarantee, and the odds hadn't ever been in her favor.

"You know he's one of the most eligible bachelors in town," Abby said, her tone laced with suggestion.

Was it true? Hannah felt a little queasy at the thought of other women pining for him. He was hers. Or he'd been hers. A long time ago.

"Of course, he seems to have no interest in dating," Abby continued, as they approached the bar that was set up just outside the room where they would all sit down for dinner soon. She ordered them two champagne cocktails and doled them out. She took a sip of hers, grinning with approval, before continuing. "They say that Alicia just ran off and left him with that little girl. It was three months before that poor child's hair was brushed for school, and one time Bridget saw the two of them at Angie's and Lucy was wearing her pajamas!"

Hannah couldn't help but grin. Yep, that sounded like Dan all right. But it sounded a lot like someone else too. It sounded like her father. She could still remember the way he'd scrambled after her mother had left. The way he forgot things like bi-annual dentist appointments that first year, and her dance recital dress rehearsal, which meant she couldn't be in the show, and, of course, little less important things like hair brushing.

Eventually, he could not only pull Hannah's hair into a ponytail, but he could braid it too.

"Of course, certain people around town see this sort of thing they become more determined than ever to fix him up," Abby said with a laugh. "All he needs is a women's touch, that's what they say. Well, I'm sure they'll be satisfied to see that he has you on his arm. For the next two days, at least."

"That's the idea," Hannah said, only the more she thought about what Abby said, the worse she felt about this whole charade. Was Dan's life really such a struggle? Did he really want to be alone so badly that he would use her as an excuse to silence anyone from setting him up for real?

He must be still in love with Alicia. It was the only conclusion.

With a heavy step, they made their way back to the group, just in time for everyone to take their seats for dinner.

Dan and Hannah were seated with a mix of family members, including Margo and her husband Eddie, and Mimi. Hannah greeted her pretend grandmother with a kiss on the cheek and then took a seat beside her and her pretend date.

She could almost smile at how ridiculous this was. Almost.

Margo was looking at her with wide-eyed interest and a curl of her mouth that said Hannah would have some explaining to do, and quickly. But it was Mimi who was surveying everything with a disapproving eye.

"Are they planning to reuse these centerpieces on Saturday?" Mimi asked no one in particular.

"No, at the wedding, Bridget is going with something a little lighter, since the reception will be in a tent."

"A big to-do for a second wedding, if you ask me," Mimi remarked, and Margo's eyes shot to Hannah's.

Hannah covered her mouth with a napkin, and felt Dan give her a little kick under the table. So this wouldn't be as bad as she'd feared. No stilted conversation. No pretending. They'd sit and eat and Mimi would complain and then it would be time to leave.

And one more night with Dan would be behind her. A thought that should relieve her but instead just saddened her.

"Well, Bridget eloped for her wedding to Ryan," Margo tried to explain, but she looked uncomfortable as she picked up her glass.

"Mimi, I just realized that you haven't introduced me to your husband!" Hannah smiled at the sweet-looking man in the bow tie who was sitting to Mimi's other side.

"Don't mind me! When you get to be my age, you'll forget your manners, too. Earl, this is Hannah. She is Anne's brother's daughter."

"The therapist?" Earl frowned, as if trying to place her.

"No, that's Evie," Mimi corrected. "Evie is the smart one. And Hannah is the pretty one."

Hannah choked on her water, thankful that Evie had been seated at another table. "Oh, now, Evie's very pretty."

Mimi looked at her frankly. "Evie is married to her books and her studies. Although, come to think about it, she did take off those glasses and make a bit of an effort tonight."

"Evie is a very accomplished young woman," Margo said, rising to Evie's defense. "All of us are!"

Hannah grew silent, thinking this wasn't exactly true. Margo had her own interior design business, Bridget was running an inn, and Abby was the cook at that inn. And Evie was pouring drinks, and Hannah...

"Not Hannah," Mimi commented. "You know she got

sacked from that fancy job."

"I just got a new job, actually," Hannah said, feeling prouder than she should probably feel, considering the new job paid less than a third what her last one did, and had no benefits either.

Evie was working her way past their table, and stopped. "You didn't mention it to me!"

"I didn't have the chance." Hannah looked up at her, feeling strangely guilty. It hadn't occurred to her to share her news with Evie. She wasn't the one that Hannah had run to in a long time. "I'll be working as a photographer for the *Gazette*." She turned to Dan, struggling to look at that square strong jaw, the straight nose, and those eyes that seemed to hold a hundred memories in them. "Thank you. For the suggestion."

"I'm glad it worked out," he said, giving her an easy grin.

"Me too," Evie said tightly, as she walked away to find her table.

Hannah watched her go, feeling the distance grow between them, and then, with a sigh, looked back at Dan. He eyed her carefully. "So does that mean you'll be sticking around town for a while then?"

She pulled in a breath. "That's the plan," she said. Only because there was no other plan.

"I'm happy to hear that," he said, his gaze turning more serious as his smile slipped.

Hannah blinked, not knowing how to respond or how

she should even feel about that, and looked away.

It didn't matter if Dan was happy she was back. Or if he was still his same, sweet self. It didn't change anything. Some things just were what they were.

*

By the time dessert was served, Evie was ready to call it a night. Her feet were killing her—she should have known better than to wear brand-new strappy sandals to an event—and she'd slipped them off her heel halfway through the main course.

But now people were starting to push back their chairs, and the mingling was starting again. With extreme reluctance, she reached down and attempted to cram her foot back into the shoe, a searing pain shooting straight up her leg when she dared to put any weight on it.

She glanced desperately around the room for her dad. He was her ride, and she could only hope he was ready to turn in. But no, she realized with a sigh. He was talking with the happy couple, laughing at something Jack was saying, and who was she to interrupt their fun?

She wondered wryly if this was why she had never been invited to any parties in college. Was she a party pooper? A dud?

Basically.

She hobbled toward the lounge area, where she'd at least have another excuse to sit, when the pain turned to fire and her ankle gave way and she slipped.

"Whoa there!" She felt two strong arms breaking her

fall and setting her upright.

Her face aflame, she turned, already muttering her gratitude amidst a mixture of excuses and locked eyes with a face she had never seen before, not even tonight, and she'd spent the last two hours observing the room, noticing little behaviors, like when Hannah scooted her chair to the left when Dan tried to sit a little closer. That had been telling. Quite telling, really.

She swallowed hard, suddenly at a loss for words as she stared up at the strange man.

"One too many, eh?" He grinned, and his eyes—a shade of deep navy blue that matched his tie—dear God, they sparkled.

One too many? If he was referring to the club sodas she'd been drinking all night, then maybe. But she had just slipped, and being tipsy was a considerably easier explanation than admitting that the skin on your heels was now turning into blisters the size of quarters.

"What can I say? It's a good party." She smiled, and it came a little easier now.

"Are you headed over there?" The man motioned to the cluster of small couches and armchairs near the oversized hearth, where a fire blazed even though it was late August and the temperature had been high, even for the season.

She nodded gratefully, imagining how good it would feel to sink into one of those chairs and take the weight off her feet until her father was ready to leave. But come to think of it, she hadn't really noticed the pain for a minute now, not since she'd discovered those twinkling eyes and that smile...

He walked with her toward the chairs, and for a moment she thought he would just leave her there, his good deed done, but instead he grabbed two glasses of wine from a waitress passing a tray and joined her on one of the smaller couches.

"To a good party," he said, clinking her glass.

To a good party, indeed, Evie thought, taking a long sip from her glass. It took the flush right out of her cheeks, despite the heat from the crackling flames beside her.

"Whose side are you on, the bride or the groom?"

"Bride," she said. "Bridget is my cousin."

"I'm here for Jack. We knew each other in New York."

Ah, so he was just in town for the wedding, which explained why she'd never seen him before. "Staying at the Oyster Bay Hotel?" she asked, kicking herself for not having anything more witty to say.

"Only for a couple weeks. I'm making something of a vacation of it. Room service is a guilty pleasure." He grinned, and if she didn't know better, she might say her stomach flip-flopped.

Since when did that happen? She'd had a boyfriend before, contrary to what most people in town thought. She'd dated her lab partner for two years in grad school, even if by the end of their relationship they did spend more time silently studying together rather than going out to movies or a restaurant. Their relationship had been solid for the most part, though, built on a common interest. But this? This was new. All new. And she wasn't so sure how she felt about it.

"So, cousin of the bride, do you have a name?" The man grinned again, and Evie wondered if he was just being polite. After all, this was a party, and she was, well, choosing to be a wallflower. She wondered if she should release him. Tell him she was fine now and set him free.

"Evie," she said.

"And what do you do, Evie?"

She considered this for a moment, and then thought, what the hell? "I'm a bartender." It was the truth, at least for now, and it was about time she accepted her current circumstances. Besides, it was a lot easier than trying to explain the long and disappointing path that had brought her to this point.

"Interesting," he said, his grin one of amusement now. "And here I had you pegged for something more like..."

Please don't say librarian. Or medical researcher. Or actuary. She'd heard all these assumptions before, especially when she wore her hair in a bun and didn't bother to swap her glasses for contacts.

But tonight her hair was down at her shoulders and she'd actually borrowed some of Hannah's makeup, feeling silly the entire time but knowing that if she was going to attend a party, she may as well play the part...

"A yoga instructor." He raked his gaze over her and Evie felt the wine go straight to her head and, even though she was sitting down and leaning against a lovely down throw pillow covered in a thick chenille fabric, she wondered for one panicked moment if she might actually faint.

She laughed instead. A little shrilly. "Nope...just a bartender. My dad owns The Lantern." Everyone knew The Lantern. Even handsome tourists.

"Well, Evie, perhaps I'll stop in for a drink sometime then," he said, giving her a grin. "I'm Liam, by the way."

Liam. That was all she knew. That he was Liam. From New York. And that he was gorgeous.

"I should probably go make the rounds," he said a little apologetically.

"Of course!" Of course he'd want to go. He'd given her enough of his time.

"Save a dance for me tomorrow night, will you?" he said, giving her a lopsided grin as he stood.

Hannah would have had a good comeback for that one. Something suave and casual and just evasive enough to leave them hanging. But Evie wasn't Hannah. Never could be. Even if she was wearing Hannah's lipstick.

"Will do," she said with a grin, and she turned toward the fire, watching the crackling flames, and she suddenly didn't care if her father wanted to stay and chat for another hour. She'd be right here. Replaying what just happened.

And analyzing it to pieces.

*

Hannah stood near the bar, nursing a glass of water and only half listening to something her oldest friend Melanie Dillon was saying.

There was a long pause, and Hannah had the distinct feeling that Melanie was waiting for her to say something.

She looked guiltily back at her friend. "I'm sorry, Melanie. I'm a little distracted at the moment."

"Would it have anything to do with the fact that Dan Fletcher can't take his eyes off you?" Melanie asked coyly. "I still can't believe you're back together."

"We're not back together. We're just here together," Hannah said, wishing she could explain the situation but knowing that certain matchmakers were within earshot.

"And you're coming to the wedding together?" Melanie asked. When Hannah nodded, she sighed and said, "And I'll be stuck at the singles table. How depressing is that?"

Hannah had heard all about Melanie's recent heartache, and her Valentine's Day timed break-up was another reminder of why it was foolish to fall in love at all. She patted Melanie's wrist. "Don't give up hope," she said, even though she'd given up hope herself.

Or maybe, she'd just faced reality.

"You either," Melanie said. "Just because my love life is nonexistent doesn't mean yours should be too." She looked over at Dan and then back at Hannah. "He's the most eligible bachelor in town, but I'd never go for him, so you don't have to worry. Poor guy was real torn up after Alicia left."

Torn up. Hannah kept her expression neutral, but inside, her heart felt like it was breaking all over again.

"Well," she said, suddenly eager to leave, "I should probably go find Evie. My dad's already outside and it's getting late."

She gave Melanie a quick hug and slipped out the nearest door, the warm ocean breeze doing little to lift her spirits. The crowd had thinned and she scanned the veranda, looking for her father, hoping that he was as ready to go as she was.

But the only familiar face she saw was Dan.

"You can't keep running off on me if we're going to pull this off," he said.

"I didn't run off on you," she reminded him. "I don't run off on people." But she had, in a way, without even realizing it. She'd run off on her father, and her sister.

There was a sadness in his eyes. "No," he said flatly, and Hannah wondered if she had hit a nerve, made him think about Alicia, about the person he'd spent far more time with than he'd ever spent with her. A woman he had lived with. Had a child with.

"It's late," she said, backing away from him. She needed space. She needed distance to stop these feelings and memories from flooding back. "I need to find my father."

"I had a good time tonight," Dan said, and something

in the way his voice lowered to something gruff and a little surprised made her feel uneasy.

She didn't want to say the same, even if she was partly in agreement. Tonight hadn't been so bad. Definitely could have been worse. There were no awkward silences. Not even angry ones. Instead there was…familiarity. Understanding. Maybe even a bit of connection.

"I should go find my dad," she said, backing away toward the door. "He's my ride and I'm sure Evie's been ready to go for like, an hour."

He said nothing more, just watched her go back inside, and for a moment she had a strange urge to stay, have another drink, put the wall down and let herself slip back to that time and place where her world was right.

Instead she walked with more purpose than ever toward her sister, who of course was sitting by herself, staring at the fire in the hearth. No doubt that was an ice water in her hands.

Evie had never known the pain of loss. She'd never wished for more than she had.

And Hannah envied her for it.

Chapter Nine

Hannah was grateful that it was Saturday because Dan didn't work on weekends, at least, that was what her dad had said on the drive home last night, somewhat suggestively if Hannah didn't know better. She turned off her alarm and slept until a warm glow of sun filled her room, the brightness of it letting her know that it was easily midmorning. But then, it had been a late night.

And it hadn't ended when her father had pulled his ancient Jeep to a stop at the back of the house and they had all emerged, tired and feet sore, knowing the day ahead would be long and they all needed to get straight to bed. Hannah had waited her turn for the upstairs bathroom, brushed her teeth, crawled into bed, and let the salty air breeze in through the open window. But unlike her father, whose snores could be heard across the hall, or Evie, who no doubt dutifully went to sleep as she knew she should, Hannah stared at the ceiling and tried to remember every detail of the night almost as much as she tried to forget.

Dan Fletcher was back in her life. The past two trips to Oyster Bay she had been committed to avoiding him, and she had. But now that she'd let him back in, no matter the pretense, she felt shaky and off balance. She had a dreamless sleep, and she was grateful for it. Her mind was overloaded.

She'd be damned if she allowed the same to happen to her heart.

She sighed and looked at the clock. She'd slept the morning away, but she was still tired. She stumbled downstairs, half expecting to find her father in the kitchen, where he was usually stationed on Saturday mornings, back when she was a kid, flipping pancakes and singing songs he made up on the spot that made them giggle when they were little and cringe as they got older, but the only person at the old oak table was Evie, sipping coffee and staring out the window. Her blonde hair was pulled back in a neat ponytail and her thick-framed glasses made her look like she was ready to hit the school library, not attend a wedding in a few short hours.

She looked out of place amidst the clutter and disarray. Evie was a neat freak. A mess like this would usually send her over the edge.

"Where's Dad?" Hannah asked as she went to open a cabinet for a mug and realized that there were no cabinets. There wasn't even a center island anymore. The coffeepot was plugged in to a jack on the floor.

"Mugs are in the dining room," Evie offered. She waited until Hannah had returned with one to say, "Dad's at the restaurant overseeing his catering staff for tonight."

Hannah looked around for cream and sugar and finally gave up. She dropped into a chair across from her sister and pushed aside a box of crackers. Her sister had a funny look on her face. A gleam in her eye that had been there the whole car ride home last night, too, come to think of it.

"Did you have fun last night?" Hannah hadn't seen much of Evie once they arrived. They hadn't been seated together, and even when there was a chance to mingle, Evie was strangely absent. Probably hiding in the bathroom, reading a book. She'd done that at every fall dance, and when Hannah finally asked why she bothered to go, Evie said that it brought so much joy to their father to see her participating that she didn't want to cause him unnecessary worry. So she brought a book and sat in a stall and everyone was happy.

Hannah's heart pulled at the memory. Their dad had always wanted the best for them. Even if what he wanted and what they wanted were two very different things.

Evie shrugged in response to Hannah's question. A strange, noncommittal shrug, and Hannah couldn't help but feel disappointed. She'd hoped that they were getting somewhere after their conversation on the roof the other night. She'd hoped that they were making progress. But it was clear that Evie was still hurt. She hadn't forgiven her yet.

And coming back here…maybe she shouldn't have. Maybe she should have just crashed on a friend's couch in San Francisco, looked for a job there.

But no. Staying in California would have been a hundred times worse. San Francisco was where she'd gone to find family, and failed. And Oyster Bay…Well, it was where she'd failed her family.

This was her mess to clean up. And she'd stay in town at least long enough to make sure she had.

"Well, today will be fun," she tried again, even though she wasn't so sure it would be any fun at all. Not just a night but half the afternoon with Dan…It was wearing on her.

"It will be!" Evie said with surprising enthusiasm. Since when did Evie look forward to parties, even if they were weddings? "I'll grab the first shower," she said, and quickly carried her mug to the sink before disappearing into the hall.

Hannah frowned after her. Something was definitely up with that girl. It wasn't like Evie to be so perky, or so optimistic. Well, whatever it was, she had time to find out. All the time in the world, as things were turning out. She was back in town, no plans or means to leave anytime soon, and now that she'd been forced back into seeing Dan, what real reason was there to run now?

She pulled her phone out of her pocket. She hadn't checked it since she'd been back. Hadn't wanted to. But now, curiosity had gotten the better of her. Had her mother reached out? Did she know that she was back in Oyster Bay?

Hannah opened her email and scanned it, and then went to her messages and did the same. She hated the disappointment that settled in her gut. Her mother hadn't reached out since she'd left California, and that was a year ago. Why would she suddenly do so now?

Kelly had been in touch. They'd never lost touch. When Hannah was in South America they kept each other up to date, sent photos, Kelly talked about a boyfriend. But now that Hannah was back in Maine, she felt strange about talking to Kelly. This was her home. Her family. And Kelly was part of another life.

"Your turn!" Evie called from upstairs, and Hannah quickly turned off her email, almost grateful for the interruption. She took a large gulp of her coffee and put it in the sink. Then she left her phone on the counter and went upstairs to shower. A shower would sober her. And she desperately needed a clear head.

By the time she came back downstairs, feeling energized and refreshed, Evie was at the table.

"Dad walked to work this morning so we could use the car. Said the exercise was good for him, but I think that was just Dad being Dad."

Of course it was, Hannah thought sadly. "Want me to drive?"

Evie nodded. "I haven't driven a car in years. Didn't need one in Boston."

It had been a year since she'd driven a car—in South America she took the bus, sometimes even hitched a ride when she made friends who were passing through, or on extended vacations—but it came naturally.

"God, this thing brings back memories," she said as she sat behind the wheel, her camera secure on Evie's lap. The feel of the leather under her hands brought her to a time and place where she was carefree, where the windows were down and the wind was whipping her hair and the radio was blaring.

Now, there was silence in the car, too much of it for Hannah's liking, and even the radio wasn't helping. Are you still mad at me, Evie? she wanted to ask. Just talk to me, tell me. Isn't that what you therapists do? Talk to people? Communicate?

But Evie just stared out the window with that dreamy look on her face.

By the time they got to Chez Moi, the day spa owned by Amanda Quinn, a former classmate, Hannah had never been more grateful to see her cousins.

Abby waved a bright blue nail polish at her. "I was going to pick this for myself, but I know it's your favorite color."

"Thanks," Hannah said, taking the bottle. She looked around the room. Margo and Emma were already sitting in massage chairs, Emma looking quite proud to be included with the grown-ups, but there was no sign of the bride to be. "Where's Bridget? I was hoping to snap a few shots of her getting ready."

"Out back. Said she needed some air. I think she's nervous," Abby confided, coming closer as she lowered her voice. "And who could blame her after what happened with Ryan?"

A thought more sobering than her cold shower had been. She'd forgotten how small the hot water tank was in that house, just like she was forgetting how easily love could end. Really, what had she been thinking, fantasizing about Dan last night? She'd been burned. Just like Bridget had been burned. Only Bridget was left to be a single parent.

Like Dan, she thought.

Oh, stop it! She scolded herself, gritted her teeth, and must have frowned quite a bit, because Abby's expression turned perplexed.

"Don't worry too much," she laughed, touching Hannah's wrist. "Knowing Bridget, she'll be all smiles and tears of joy by the time they start her makeup, and then they'll have to wipe it off and start all over."

Hannah mumbled something of agreement under her breath and followed Abby over to the row of chairs, where Evie was already sitting next to Margo, her feet in a pool of bubbling water.

Hannah looked sharply at the nail polish bottle her sister held in her hand. Was that an actual color? Since she'd been a teenager, Evie's wardrobe consisted of three colors: black, grey, and beige. Her nails were clear. Pale pink at best.

"What?" Evie was prickly, and Hannah realized she had been gawking at her.

"Nothing," Hannah said, but that wasn't true at all. Something, yes, something was certainly going on with her sister, and it had nothing to do with her tension with Hannah.

"So you're coming with Dan again tonight?" Margo asked Hannah, leaning to see her across Evie, who seemed just as curious by all this as her cousins were.

"Just as old friends," Hannah said lightly, but her heart was starting to race and she feared her face would soon flame. She sank her feet into the water at the base of her chair, focused on the bubbles. Not the heat.

"You two looked pretty cozy to me last night." Margo waggled her eyebrows, and Evie narrowed her eyes as a strange smile curved her mouth.

"It's not like that. But it beats having to dance with Timmy Wright tonight!" Hannah laughed, feeling awkward when no one's expression changed.

"Look at me and Zach," Abby pointed out. "And Margo and Eddie. We've all had a second chance."

A second chance. Was there really a possibility of the same outcome for her and Dan?

The answer to that was a firm no. Dan wasn't interested in dating. Everyone had said so. And Hannah wasn't either. So good thing that much was clear. No second chance.

As if they even existed.

*

Evie spotted Liam as soon as she took her seat at the ceremony. He was across the aisle, on the groom's side, two rows up, where he wouldn't able to see her staring at him.

Staring was the wrong word, she decided. She was observing.

Actually, she was admiring. Yes, that was the correct word if she was being completely honest with herself.

She sighed. Stood when the procession started. Smiled at the joy in Bridget's face as she walked down the aisle. Evie's father had offered to walk Bridget down the aisle, and he'd done the same for Margo when she married Eddie in the spring. Did it bother him that he was yet to walk either of his own daughters down the aisle? If it did, he wouldn't say so. Her father had always been sensitive that way, and she loved him for it.

Evie took her seat again, grinning at the gleam in little Emma's eye as she studied the crowd and then looked up at her mother and then back at her dress, a frothy pink confection that clearly made her feel very special. It sent a pang straight to her heart when she saw interactions like this. Sweet, tender moments between a mother and daughter. Moments that she'd never had.

She pushed the thought away as quickly as it entered. She'd made an easy habit of it over the years. Good, hard work was the best distraction. Observing others was another. She focused on the bride and the groom all through the short yet beautiful ceremony, until the vows were sealed with a kiss and the guests erupted into applause.

By the time she followed everyone up from the beach to the tent that had been set up on the lawn for the reception, she'd lost track of Liam in the crowd, and with a heavy heart, found her place card and made her way to what was clearly the singles table.

Melanie Dillon was already seated, looking a little morose and well into the wine. Evie had always been fond of her, even if she was closer in age and friendship with Hannah. Beside her was a pretty girl named Sarah Preston, who had recently moved to Oyster Bay and worked at the *Gazette*. And then there was Tim Wright, awkward as ever, his mother stage whispering to him from the next table to sit a little straighter, gesturing to him with wide eyes and a pinched mouth when he didn't immediately follow her command.

And then, suddenly, there was Liam.

His gaze swept over the table, lingering on her for just a moment. He gave a wide grin as he pulled out his chair. "Hello, everyone."

"Hello!" Melanie batted her eyelashes in a way that made Evie immediately feel both proprietary and depressed all at once.

Melanie was pretty. And easy to talk to. Okay, she'd put on a bit of weight—rumor had it on account of a bad break-up last winter—but she was curvy in all the right places. And even though Evie had made a special effort tonight, she couldn't help but feel like she was playing a part.

She looked down at the bright pink paint that colored her nails and then, feeling extremely self-conscious, pulled her hands down into her lap.

This wasn't her. She wasn't Evie, the cool, breezy bartender who wore strapless dresses borrowed from her sister's closet, even if they did make Hannah seem suspicious, and shoes that made her feet bleed. She was Evie, the girl who took far more pleasure in a Saturday night with a stack of books and a pot of tea and comfortable and practical flannel pajama pants.

Liam probably thought this Evie wore lingerie to bed.

Miserable, she frowned at Melanie, whose smile was wide and whose eyes were dazzling.

Well, what harm was there in letting him think so? Maybe someday she would own lingerie. Maybe, she'd even wear it.

"Hello!"

Fabulous. Now Melanie's cousin Chloe had arrived. Chloe was chic and elegant and, along with Melanie, ran a bridal salon. She was a smart business woman. She was self-made. She hadn't worked her entire life only to be told she hadn't joined enough extracurricular activities to pursue the career she'd aspired to! No, Chloe was well-rounded. She'd been on student council. She'd joined the clubs and committees. She'd cheered at all the football games. With pom poms!

And now Chloe was sitting beside Liam. Why did Evie bother swapping out her glasses for contacts?

She reached for her champagne, suddenly realizing why people reached for a drink. It took the edge off, didn't it? But wait, was he…looking at her? And was he leaning over the table and saying something to Tim, and were they suddenly standing, and were there chairs moving? And was Mrs. Wright watching all of it with alarm in her eyes, only finally relaxing when Tim took a seat between Chloe and Sarah, two cute blondes.

Evie slowly drifted her gaze to her left, where Liam was now sitting beside her, a grin on his face. "That's better."

She blinked, not even knowing what to say.

"Looks like today's my lucky day," he said as he unfolded his napkin and set it in his lap. "You never know how the singles table will go." And then, just when she thought she needed to be properly pinched and woken up, he winked at her.

Evie was acutely aware of the wide-eyed stares from all the other women at the table as she reached for her water glass and took a sip. She was nervous. More nervous than she'd been when she'd gone for the big interview at the hospital, because back then she actually felt confident that her transcript would speak for itself. Shop talk she could do. But casual banter with a good-looking guy? Not her territory.

She took a steadying breath and told herself to treat him like a patient. People loved to talk about themselves, and she was an excellent listener.

But before she had a chance to ask him what he did for a living, he turned the tables on her. "What do people do for fun around here?"

She startled, then calmed herself. This was an easy one. She could do this. "Oh, there's the beach, of course. And some historic sites, like the old lighthouse. And the shops in town."

"Seen them all," he said, dismissing that one. "How about the beach? Want to show me the best spot tomorrow?"

Oh, dear God, he was actually asking her out. And she had promised her father she'd work from noon to four. And she was never one to let her father down. Unlike Hannah.

"I have to work tomorrow afternoon," she said, her tone a mix of both regret and relief. A formal event surrounded by others she knew she could handle, but one on one with this man? Entirely too much pressure. More pressure than midterm exams. You could study for those. You could not study for a date.

A date. That was really what he was implying!

"After your shift then," he said with a good-natured grin, and really, how could she resist that?

"Okay," she said weakly. "I work at The Lantern."

"I remember."

He remembered! Her heart was beating faster now. She swallowed back the panic that was rising in her throat. "My shift ends at four."

"I'll be there at four then," he said, and before Evie could open her mouth to protest, there was a tapping of a glass and a man was standing up and it was time for the toasts to begin.

Evie settled back into her chair and relished in the silence for a moment. And despite being a good listener, she didn't absorb a single word of the speeches. She was far too busy taking mental inventory of her closet, and wondering what she should wear to work the next day.

Chapter Ten

It was a beautiful wedding, but then Hannah had no doubts. Every personal touch, every flower, every tear, every secret smile, made for a camera-ready moment. Hannah knew that she had captured the emotion of the event, and it made her heart sing to know that Bridget would look back on these photos for years to come and remember all the love that had gone into the day.

Jesus, she was turning into a real sap, wasn't she? Who knew weddings could have this effect on her? She'd blame it on the champagne except she was strictly avoiding it for today. She didn't drink on the job. Besides, she needed a clear head to deal with Dan.

Last night had been confusing. Tonight there would be no gray area.

"There you are."

She turned to see Dan standing behind her, a shy smile on his face that pulled at something deep within her. It reminded her of the first time he'd asked her out. It had been to a school dance, of all things, the first of the year. It was a crisp fall day and she'd been sitting outside, reading a book in the gazebo of the town square after school, and then, there he was. Danny Fletcher, looking adorable and bashful all at once. Sure, she'd known him all her life. Been in school with him since they were playing with building blocks. But he'd changed over the summer. Grown. His voice was deep, and he even had a hint of facial hair. He'd always been a nice boy, one that had risen to her defense the time that Timmy Wright had climbed under the bleachers and stared up her skirt in sixth grade. She hadn't forgotten that. Danny was a gentleman. He was kind. And now he was standing here, looking nervous as hell, his hands in his pockets, his smile a little hesitant.

"Hey," he'd said, and something told her that he'd come for a reason. After all, what was there to suddenly be shy about? They'd known each other all their lives!

"Hey," she said, smiling up at him as she set her book to the side. She stared at him patiently, wondering what he was up to.

"So there's a dance this Friday. You going?"

She'd shrugged. She'd planned to go with Melanie Dillon, her best friend that year, since they'd both trained as junior camp counselors at the beach camp that summer. "Probably," she said, as it dawned on her that he might be there too, and he might even ask her to dance. She and Melanie had already gone shopping for their dresses. Melanie bought something red and slinky and very age inappropriate. Hannah bought a vintage teal dress with an A-line skirt and gold pumps.

"I was thinking that maybe we could...go together." His brand new Adam's apple seemed to roll in his throat, and Hannah's heart had started to beat so quickly that she was nearly sure he could hear it.

"Okay," she said.

His eyes shot open in surprise for one telling second, and then that slow grin returned. "Okay," he said.

They smiled at each other for one long second, and then he left. And she picked up her book. But she didn't read a word on the page. She just kept thinking that Danny Fletcher had gotten awfully cute over the summer. And that he'd asked her to the dance. And that the world felt full of possibility.

Now Dan was looking at her with that same sweet smile, his eyes steady but unsure, and her heartstrings pulled in a way she didn't want them to anymore. Not for Dan. Not for anyone, really.

"If you keep hiding from me, old Beverly Wright might get the wrong idea and try to set you up with Peepin' Tim again."

He gestured across the dance floor, where sure enough, Bev was watching their interaction with wide eyes, one hand on her son's wrist.

Hannah couldn't help but smile. "Aw, Timmy. Think he'll ever find Miss Right? No pun intended."

"There's someone for everyone, I suppose," Dan said with a shrug. There was a hint of nostalgia to his tone that made her wonder if he was thinking about his ex-wife. Or…her.

Nonsense! "You really believe that?" Once she would have said so. But she'd seen too much heartbreak over time to believe that anymore.

She looked him square in the eye, hating the fact that it hurt to do so. She felt like she was looking into the past, into a hundred lazy days that she'd taken for granted. That when their eyes met, he was remembering too. And maybe, like her, regretting.

"You mean to tell me that you're here, at a wedding, and you don't believe in everlasting love?"

She considered it for about two seconds and then said, "That's right."

He blinked, the sadness in his expression brief before a guilty smile crossed his mouth. "Have to say I'm with you. At least about the everlasting part."

Huh. So he'd turned into a brooding cynic, too? Well, weren't they just the pair? Not that they were a pair, of course. A pair implied a couple. They were more like two bruised individuals standing on the outside, looking in, knowing something about love and life that all these poor, happy for now fools hadn't discovered. Yet.

"You know, we should probably dance." Dan lifted an

eyebrow playfully.

"Dance?" She stared at him in horror. He may as well have suggested that they fling off their clothes and go skinny dipping in the ocean.

It wouldn't be the first time, she thought, with a pang of sadness that hit her every time she looked back on those carefree days. Back then they were unstoppable, and nothing gave them pause. Their summer days were spent working in their father's businesses—her as a waitress at The Lantern, him as an apprentice on job sites—and at night, they loved nothing more than to take a picnic down to the beach, talk for hours as they stretched on the warm sand, watching the sun set until the stars began to dot the night sky, and then swimming in the ocean, the warm salt water cooling their bodies, the entire world feeling like it belonged only to them.

Now she imagined other afternoons that Dan must have spent on the beach, building sandcastles with his daughter, eating the sandwiches that his wife had packed. Packing up the truck and heading back to their house farther inland, sand on the seats and the wind in their hair.

He'd lived an entire life with someone else. And yet here he was, asking her to dance as if no time had passed at all.

"I haven't danced since senior prom," she admitted, and something in her stung when he didn't say the same.

He'd probably danced at his wedding. Probably danced at other weddings he'd attended. And she'd only ever danced with him.

"Everyone's watching. No time like the present." He held out a hand and, with a sigh, she took it, surprised by how achingly familiar it was. His palms were rough, no doubt from days of hard work, but she didn't mind. His hand was warm and big and the one thing that hadn't changed about him, when it felt like so much else had.

He pulled her close, guiding her into a box step, and she tried not to breathe in his scent, or push her chest too close to his. She wanted distance. She wanted to get through this night. But she also didn't want it to end.

Tomorrow Dan would go back to his life and she would go back to hers. This was the reality she had accepted all those years ago, when she knew there was nothing she could say, that he was right, he was doing the right thing, and nothing she could say could argue that, and it would have been wrong for her to ask for anything.

The song faded out, and she stepped back. Duty done. Her job was done.

"I should probably take some more photos," she said. A perfectly good excuse to break away.

"Don't stay away from me all night," he warned. "Not unless you want the speculation to start. If they think we aren't together, the suggestions of who we should be with will be worse than ever."

Hannah considered more prying from Mrs. Wright and let out a long sigh. "I'll be sure to check back in before the last call."

"I'm thinking that we should actually just keep this going for a bit," Dan surprised her by saying.

"Excuse me?" She could only imagine what her expression looked like right now. Shock? Horror?

"No harm in letting everyone think there's something going on." He shrugged and held her eyes in challenge.

Was he daring her to admit something, that she still cared? That it bothered her to have to spend time with him?

Like she'd give him that satisfaction. Not when he'd walked away, the break clean and firm, and moved on with his life. He'd had an instant family. While she had...well, nothing, she realized, when she thought of what she'd gone after and what she'd left behind.

"Fine, but don't make a big deal out of it. It doesn't have to be some big romance. Just something...casual."

He nodded, seeming satisfied. "Enough to make them turn their attention to someone else. Lose interest."

"But not enough to make them speculate too much with us."

"Like...a future?" He cocked an eyebrow, and she narrowed her eyes at him. That was too close to home, reminding her of how deep his relationship with Alicia must have been at some point, even if it hadn't lasted.

Torn up. That's what people said. They said he was torn up since the divorce.

He'd loved Alicia. And why shouldn't he have?

But he'd loved her first. Yet somehow, that didn't seem to count so much anymore. Maybe it was who you'd loved last that really mattered.

And she'd loved him last.

Hannah felt a tug at her dress, and she looked down to see Emma staring earnestly back at her. "My mom is about to throw the bouquet," she said.

"Okay," Hannah said, giving the little girl a smile. "Are you going to try to catch it?"

"No, silly!" By her giggles, Emma clearly found this notion to be preposterous. "I'm too little. But you're old enough."

"Oh…" Hannah winced. It was one thing to attend a wedding. To actively participate was another. "I don't really think I'm up for it," she told Emma, feeling like a real jerk when she saw that Emma's expression folded in bewilderment.

"But it's such a pretty bouquet. Why don't you want to catch it?"

"Yeah, Hannah, why don't you want to catch it?" Dan's eyes were full of mirth when she leveled him with a stern look. "Emma, why don't you show Hannah where to go. I'll stay right here and watch your camera."

In other words, no excuses.

Grumbling a string of complaints under her breath, she allowed Emma to pull her by the hand to the center of the tent, where every single woman in Oyster Bay was currently lined up, including Evie, Hannah noticed in surprise.

Feeling like a fraud, she released Emma's hand on the

promise of really trying hard, fingers crossed and all that, and heaved a sigh. Hopefully it would go to Melanie. Or Abby. Yes, Abby was still technically able to catch the bouquet as she was not married or engaged.

But as Bridget released the bouquet, Hannah immediately knew that Abby would not be the one catching it. It was heading right in her direction, and unless she had time to quickly dart to the left, it would either hit the floor or be caught by her.

And she hated to let Emma down.

Hannah opened her arms, took one step forward, and with a bemused grin, caught the bouquet, sending petals in every shade of pink floating to the floor.

"You did it, you did it!" Emma cried, skipping over to her.

"I did it for you," she said, trying to hand off the bouquet to the little girl.

Emma was having none of it. "Uh-uh. I don't want to get married! When you get married you have to kiss boys!" She stuck out her tongue and made a choking sound, and this time, Hannah smiled for real. "Besides, I already have flowers. I'm the flower girl." She pointed at her dress, as if this should be obvious.

"Oh, la la!" Abby said, skipping up beside her. "Poor Sarah was really hoping to catch it, I know, but, I think it went to the rightful owner." She elbowed Hannah and gave her a wink, and this time, Hannah wasn't smiling at all.

"I should have been taking photos of that," she said

ruefully.

"Nonsense! You're a photographer and a guest. And a single woman," Abby said. She tapped the bouquet. "But maybe not for long..."

Oh, for heaven's sake! Hannah shook her head and went off in search of her camera, ignoring the gloating expression on Dan's face as she approached the table.

"Don't worry," she said, setting down the bouquet and picking up her camera. "I can assure you that I am not the marrying kind."

His eyes looked a little sad as she turned to go, and her heart pounded as she walked across the room, snapping random shots of the bride and groom dancing, their feelings for each other evident in every candid shot.

On instinct, she moved the lens of the camera back toward the bar area where Dan was still standing and frowned at the image she saw through it. He looked sad, maybe even a little nostalgic. And he wasn't looking out across the room at the other smiling couples, or even at the bride and groom.

He was looking straight at her.

Chapter Eleven

Hannah woke late, had a leisurely breakfast in the quiet, albeit messy, kitchen, and packed up her camera for the day. She supposed she could stick around the house, maybe bring a book out to the hammock in the backyard, but she was eager to get out.

It was cowardly, she knew, to be avoiding Dan one day and her father the next. As much as her relationship with Evie was strained, she was happy for her presence here in the house. It meant there was a buffer, that she didn't need to be alone with her father.

But of course right now Evie was in the shower and her father's footsteps were growing closer on the floorboards, his heavy tread always making the bottom stair creak.

"Heading out?" And there he was, her father, standing

in the doorway, a pleasant smile on his face that told her everything she already knew. He loved her. He had forgiven her. So why did that confirmation almost make her feel worse?

"I thought I'd go take some pictures while the light is good." It was a lame excuse, and the way his eyes turned flat for a moment told her that he knew it too.

"Well, don't let me keep you," he said, giving a small smile.

He opened the fridge and retrieved a bottle of orange juice. She hesitated at the door, watching him look around the room in confusion.

"The glasses are on the dining room table," she offered.

He held up a finger. "Ah. The logical place."

Hannah grinned, wondering if she should stick around, use this opportunity to do what she knew she had to do. To apologize. To explain. It hadn't been that he wasn't enough. It was that for some reason she'd needed more.

Instead she opened the door, took the steps down to the gravel drive that extended to the detached garage, and headed toward the beach, feeling bad about herself with every step and vowing that soon, very soon, she would open her mouth and do the right thing.

The right thing.

But sometimes the right thing was the hardest thing, wasn't it?

With a heaviness in her chest, she walked the short

distance to the coastline, careful as she climbed over craggy rocks not to slip in her sandaled feet. If she broke her camera, she'd have no means of fixing it, and she'd be out of the job at the paper. Tomorrow was her official start date at the Gazette. She'd be handed a list of articles that were scheduled for the week, and she had creative liberty to provide photos for each one. It was not exactly hard news. More like local happenings. Still, it was a paying gig, and it was something for her resume.

And an excuse to be out of the house.

She was just clearing the bend at Gull Point when she spotted him. Up ahead, so small that most people probably couldn't be certain, running to the water and back again, with a pink plastic bucket in his hand. She knew that stride. She knew the length of his legs. She knew the width of his shoulders. She knew how the light caught the color in his hair, turning it from brown to copper, especially in the summer.

And there, kneeling in the sand, was a child. A child with the same brown hair that was golden when the sun caught the ends. A child who was laughing and pointing as the water sloshed from the bucket. A child with the same long legs as she stood and ran over to her father.

The child that Hannah had tried every day for more than eleven years not to think about. And there she was. A living, smiling, happy being.

Hannah crouched down behind a rock and zoomed her lens in, until she could make out the little girl's face. She looked like Dan, all right. Same eyes. Same smile.

Especially when Dan sloshed her with the water in the bucket instead of pouring it into the moat of the sandcastle they were building.

Her grinned down at her, and Hannah felt her heart skip a beat, and a pain filled her chest, so deep, that she had to put her camera down for a moment. She knew that look. She'd seen it just a bit ago. It was the same look her father had given her when he'd come into the kitchen. A look of pure love. Unconditional love.

Hannah blinked, thinking of that child, the child she had once resented just for existing. For being the one thing that had changed everything for them. She stared, smiling when the girl squealed loudly and gave Dan a good hard splash of water, right in the face, and somehow, in that moment, all that sadness, and all that anger, was gone.

Dan had been happy. Dan was happy.

And much as it broke her heart that she wasn't the one to give that to him, she wouldn't want to be the one who had denied it for him. Then, or now.

*

Dan caught the image of a woman in his periphery, taking just a split second to realize that it was Hannah. He watched as she came closer, the air in his chest seeming to lock up for a minute, until a surge of cold water hit him right in the face, snapping him back to the present.

Lucy was giggling so hard she had hiccups, and

Hannah's laughter could be heard a solid ten feet away.

Dan shook the water from his hair and gave her a grin. "I blame you for this, you know."

"Me?" Hannah looked at him in surprise.

"You caught me off guard. I...didn't expect to see you here." This was one of his favorite spots on the shoreline, a place he'd been coming to since Lucy was a baby. There'd been endless afternoons of picnics and sandcastles and splashing in the waves. Sometimes, on days like this, he wanted to freeze time. Here, on the shore, they were always just father and daughter. And everything was right in the world.

He eyed Hannah carefully. It was awkward, having her here, observing him in his element. Playing a role she'd never had firsthand witness to before. She'd never met Lucy. Never inquired about her this past week. And he was sensitive enough not to mention her, even if Lucy was usually his favorite subject.

But now Hannah was looking at him, a sad smile on her face that told him that she understood, that she got it, and that maybe she was even happy for him.

"Who's that?" Lucy asked, looking up at him.

He pulled in a sigh and looked at Hannah for approval. She gave him a nod.

"This is a very special person to me, Lucy," he said, glancing at Hannah. He registered the shock in her face, the way her expression turned from surprise to resignation quicker than you could blink an eye. "She's an old friend. We used to be very close when we were younger."

"Why aren't you close anymore?" Lucy asked.

Wasn't that a loaded question? Lucy didn't know the story of her conception. Didn't know the struggle he'd faced, the choices he'd made, the sacrifices that had come with those choices. She'd known joy. And love. And laughter. All the things he'd promised himself he would give her when he committed to being the best father he could be.

And she'd made it easy. From the moment he'd seen her, she had his heart.

Hannah stepped forward, this time looking to Dan for approval. "Because I moved away. I've only just come back to town recently."

"You didn't visit?" Lucy wanted to know.

Hannah gave a sheepish smile. "A bit. But it's been a while."

The answer seemed to satisfy Lucy, and she picked up her bucket and went off in search of shells.

"I don't want—" He stopped. He didn't know what he wanted to say to Hannah. Not really. That he was sorry. So sorry. But for breaking her heart, not for making his choice. That he'd missed her. Because he had. He'd missed her every damn day. That he hoped to hell this wasn't awkward, even though it was, for him at least.

"She's beautiful, Dan," Hannah interrupted, and she reached out to squeeze his wrist, her smile brave but sincere.

He nodded, knowing it was true just as much as it probably hurt Hannah to say so. Lucy was beautiful, inside and out. She was worth every hardship, every tear, every doubt he'd ever had.

"She's my world," he said, putting it out there.

"As she should be," Hannah said, nodding. She looked down, dragging a foot through the sand. When she looked back up at him, her eyes glimmered. "You made the right choice."

"Hannah." He frowned at her, but she didn't frown back. She just smiled, that beautiful smile that she hadn't given just for him since he was just a boy, but her eyes shone with tears.

"No, I mean it. Look at her. She adores you. This is…how it should be." She let out a shaky breath, and motioned to her camera. "Do you mind?"

"Be my guest!" He was never good with a camera, and since Alicia had left, he had few opportunities for a photo of him and Lucy together. She was in to selfies now, and he'd tried to get in on that, but he never looked at the right place on the phone, meaning the photo always ended with him looking at the sky, or off to the left, and she always clucked her tongue and rolled her eyes when she saw the results.

She snapped a few of Lucy, playing in the sand, and then said, "Go join her. And act natural."

Natural. What was natural about this? The only girl he'd ever loved finally meeting the only other girl he'd ever loved? Two separate lives that should never have been able to cross paths, but thanks to Alicia's departure, somehow could.

He stood beside his daughter, the water lapping at their feet, and reached down to hold her hand, his heart warming when she took hold of it, looked up at him, and gave him a brilliant smile.

Yep. Worth all of it. Every damn thing.

"Perfect," Hannah said, looking at the screen of her camera. She started moving up toward the dock that led into town. "Well, I should get going, I don't want to interrupt."

He realized that he didn't want her to go. That he wanted her to stay here. Talk to her. Just a little bit longer.

"Why don't we have dinner one night this week? For old times' sake?" Shoot. He'd pushed too far. Her gaze was hesitant, and she was chewing on her lip. Quickly, he added, "We have to keep up the ruse, after all. Unless, you prefer a dinner with Timmy?"

Hannah laughed, and shook her head. "You should have been on the debate team."

"I would have been. If I hadn't been spending every afternoon with you," he said quietly.

Their eyes met, for one, brief second, and he knew she was thinking about the past just as much as he was.

"Fine. Dinner."

He did a quick calculation before she changed her mind. Or maybe, before he changed his. "You free Tuesday?"

She backed away, tossing her arms in the air, but she was smiling. "Tuesday it is, I guess!"

Tuesday, he thought, as he watched her walk away. He could hardly wait.

*

As feared, Ron had indeed spent a few nights in jail. Evie listened to his entire story with a worried frown, waiting for him to finish before chiming in. There were only two other customers at the bar; the big crowd wouldn't hit until her shift was over. When she was at the beach with Liam.

A flutter rippled through her stomach and it had nothing to do with the titillating part of Ron's story, where he followed Jill to Dave's house, hid in the bushes for a good long peek in the windows, and then, without even bothering to check if the front door was unlocked, busted it in with his shoulder and announced his arrival.

"Didn't we decide it would be better for you to stay on the boat until she was out of the house?" Evie asked with a lift of her eyebrow.

Ron gave her a sheepish look. "I couldn't help myself. I couldn't stop thinking about it. I had to follow her."

"But you already knew where she was going." Even if it hadn't been where she'd told him she was going.

"But she lied to me. I'm not going to let her make a fool out of me!"

Evie gestured to the sling that was wrapped around his neck. "And was dislocating your shoulder and spending two nights in jail worth it?"

He gave her a wicked grin. "Yes, ma'am."

She sighed. Then who was she to argue? She could advise. She could listen. But this was ultimately his life to live, his choices to make, however poor. "Well, now that you have exorcised this torment that was distracting you from being productive, hopefully you can start moving forward in a more positive direction. I suspect you will ultimately be a lot happier on your own once you allow yourself to accept the fact that you deserve better and that you will find better."

"But I loved her," Ron said quietly. "I really, really did."

"I know," Evie said softly. She reached below the bar and pulled out the box of tissues she now kept on hand for moments like this. Earlier today she'd listened to a girl tell her about the boy who broke up with her (without reason, so she claimed) and how she'd howled outside his apartment door for four hours, desperate for him to open it and let her in, so he could explain. But he never had. So she'd come here for a week, at the insistence of a friend, who quickly formed a connection with a bartender at Dunley's, and was now nowhere to be found.

Ah, love. It really was a complicated thing, she was discovering. Not that she'd ever really had firsthand experience. Yet.

Her father poked his head out of the kitchen door, and Evie knew her cue. She patted Ron's hand and untied her apron strings. "Remember, you have to love yourself first and foremost. Think of all your attributes. I'm sure you'll come up with a lot of them. Make a list!"

Ron sniffed and plucked another tissue from the box as her father's eyes rounded in alarm.

"Are you manning the bar or running a damn group therapy session out there, Evie?" he asked once the kitchen door had swung shut behind her.

Evie jutted her chin in defiance. "I'm just listening."

Chip's mouth thinned. "Well, I don't know whether you're good for business or bad for it. We're picking up more afternoon business than usual. On the flip side, I've never seen so many grown men crying before!"

Evie took this as a compliment and hung her apron on the hook. "Well, my shift is up in two minutes. I, uh, might be late tonight."

"No problem. Out with your cousins?" Chip turned his attention to an inventory list that the head chef handed him.

Evie sighed. Of course he'd automatically assume she was doing something platonic. "Something like that," she said, as she pushed out the door and into the restaurant again.

And there he was. Just as good looking as he'd been the day before, only this time wearing a tee shirt and shorts and a grin that told her that he was looking forward to this evening just as much as she was.

If such a thing were even possible.

Chapter Twelve

When Hannah arrived home from work on Tuesday afternoon, her feet tired from an early start and a job that required more walking from location to location than she'd factored in, given her lack of a car or funding for one, she'd assumed the dinner that Dan had proposed wasn't happening. Disappointment met relief when his truck wasn't in the driveway, and she told herself that it was better this way. Deep down she'd hoped it would be canceled. It was why she'd headed out of the house before he arrived yesterday and today, even if work was now a handy excuse. Spending time together only allowed nostalgia to creep in. They'd gone their separate ways. What was done was done. There was no turning back the clock in life.

She opened the kitchen door with a sigh, deciding to

indulge in a much needed pint of chocolate ice cream tonight, until she remembered that as of yesterday, they officially had no fridge, and she nearly gasped when she saw Dan standing in the middle of the mess.

"What are you doing here? I mean, I didn't see your car."

"Joe took it to run some lumber down to the pier. My truck is bigger than his and it was a big order. Believe it or not, this kitchen isn't the only project on the books."

"Of course," she said, giving an uneasy smile. She tried to inch away, wondering if he'd forgotten about their plans for the evening or if he'd just come to his senses and changed his mind, when he cleared this throat, making her stop.

She turned, looked at him, and those raised eyebrows told her that he hadn't forgotten. Or changed his mind.

And she...well, she didn't quite know what to think about that.

"Joe's coming back in a bit. He's heading over to the Sweeney house after that. Building a sunroom."

"So, you'll need to give him a lift?" Please say yes, she thought. Please say that work commitments have made it impossible for us to go through with this ridiculous plan.

"Nope," he said good-naturedly. "His car's there. And he can easily walk from here."

She nodded and decided to play dumb. She just wouldn't say anything about tonight. And maybe he wouldn't either.

"Well, I should go put my camera away from all this

dust," she said, inching toward the hall. "Just got in from work and all."

"Work, great. You can tell me all about it at dinner."

"Dinner?" She stared at him, trying to gauge his thoughts on the entire thing. How could he be so casual about it?

"That's right. I have a six o'clock reservation."

But that was in less than half an hour. "I…need to change."

He just nodded and leaned against a set of new cabinets that were missing their countertops. "I can wait."

With her teeth on edge, Hannah left the room, took the stairs to her bedroom, and set her camera on the dresser. Right now Danny Fletcher was downstairs waiting to take her to dinner, just like he used to do when they were eighteen years old. Back then he and Chip would talk about sports while she took her time brushing her hair, choosing her dress.

Today she flung on jeans and a tank top, matching Dan's equally casual attire. No need to send the wrong message. After all, this wasn't a real dinner date. This was just…dinner.

Still, she brushed her hair. Just in case she bumped into Mimi.

Dan was already outside when she emerged a few minutes later, his truck back in its usual spot, the radio blasting through the open windows. His shirt fresh.

"Remember this song?" he asked, turning up the

volume as he drove the short distance into town.

Hannah smiled, but at the same time, tears burned the back of her eyes. She stared out the window, at the ocean in the distance, at the hydrangea bushes that were in bloom, blue petals against white picket fences. It was their song. The song they'd always sung to on their drives to the beach or the pier, the song that she hadn't been able to listen to in over a decade without feeling like her heart was being ripped out of her chest. Without wondering what might have been, and then knowing what was.

She leaned over and flicked off the radio. "I don't like that song anymore," she said.

He frowned but said nothing. She felt bad, childish even, but she was honest. She didn't like that song. Didn't like the way it made her feel. Didn't like the memories it drummed up.

What was the point of living in the past, of pining for something that never was? People had choices. Dan had made his. Just like her mother had made hers. People left. People moved on. And what was the purpose of wishing for more than what was?

By the time they arrived at the restaurant—and not just any restaurant, but the best one in town (other than The Lantern, of course)—Hannah hadn't spoken more than two words. They were seated at an outdoor table at Bistro del Mare, owned by the same family that had owned the ice cream parlor for generations. Even Chip said that no one could make a fish stew that topped the Bistro. It was a popular place, especially on summer nights, with sidewalk tables that leant a full view of Main Street and all its happenings.

Dan stared at her for a moment and then set his menu down. "You know, if you keep sulking like this, people will think we've had a lovers' quarrel, and then you'll really be getting chatted up by Beverly Wright."

She sighed. He was right. And she had agreed to come, after all.

"This isn't easy for me," she admitted, hating the way her voice betrayed her emotion.

"I know," he said quietly. "It isn't easy for me either."

"Then why did you suggest it? There must be another way to get people off our backs."

"I guess I wanted to see you again," he said, and her stomach did something funny. "I liked spending time with you. It felt good. Like old times. Before life turned complicated."

"But it is complicated," she pointed out. She couldn't feed into what he'd said. No good would come from that. "We can't go back, Dan."

"I know." He picked up his menu, and she did the same. Silence stretched and she wondered if she'd been too hard on him, but it wasn't just him she had to be firm with. She had to be firm with herself.

She heard a shuffling and glanced over to see Dottie approaching their table with a knowing smile. "And there's the happy couple. Of course, not everyone in town is as pleased by this reunion as I am, especially

Beverly Wright, but it's so nice to see the two of you together again. Of course, if it doesn't work out again this time, just knock on my door and I'll get out my Rolodex."

"Have a wonderful evening, Dottie." Dan spoke the words with a smile, but a firm one, one that said he wouldn't be engaging.

Reluctantly, Dottie walked over to her table, where she was meeting a few other women from the historical society that she headed up. All four women stared at Dan and Hannah with interest.

"Was Dottie implying that you were going to dump me again?" Hannah asked as she scanned the list of specials, shaking her head.

"You know I didn't dump you," he said.

"No." He hadn't. "But they don't know that, do they?"

Dan suddenly closed his menu and set it back on the table. "You know, I never really liked this place very much. The Lantern is much better." He pushed back his chair and stood.

She looked up at him, startled. "I thought you said we were having dinner."

"Let's give these people something new to talk about."

She stared at him in alarm, wondering just what he meant by that, but she didn't have time to speak. No sooner had she set her napkin on the table and slid back her chair, than he was taking her by the hand and pulling her toward him. Her free hand hit his chest in the same fluid motion that he leaned in to kiss her. Softly, slowly, and just long enough to send a hundred wonderful memories fluttering to the surface.

He pulled back, his eyes unreadable as she stared at him.

"Come on," he said, glancing around the room. "Let's get out of here."

She hesitated, the touch of his mouth still tingling her lips, and much as she knew it was just part of the act, that the kiss had meant nothing more than the dance at the wedding had, she nodded.

She did want to get out of the restaurant, away from prying eyes. But more than anything, she wanted to go with Dan, back to that time and place where life had felt full of hope.

*

There was only one place that Dan wanted to go. Their place. He couldn't resist it. Just like he couldn't resist cranking the volume on that stupid song. It had upset her, and he hadn't meant to upset her. It was the last thing he wanted to do.

And he would tell her that. Tonight. He'd tell her a lot of things. How he was sorry. But he wasn't sorry. How he wished things had been different just has much as he wouldn't trade them for the world. That he wanted something he couldn't have. That he wanted it all. That he'd tried. And failed. That he'd missed her.

The Clam Shack was at the north end of the beach, a seasonal joint with a limited menu that served the best fries and shakes in New England. He ordered their usual: two chocolate shakes, two fries, and two lobster rolls. They walked over to the small cove that was carved out of the craggy rocks and settled on the sand.

"I haven't been back here in years," he admitted, taking a sip of his drink.

"You don't come to the Clam Shack anymore?" Hannah asked in surprise.

"No, I meant here. The cove."

She gave him a guarded look, then reached down to unwrap her sandwich. "Well, that was a long time ago. You've had other things to think about all these years."

"True. But it doesn't mean I didn't think of you." He hesitated, wondering if there was any point in continuing, but knowing that he had to. "I always felt bad, for the way things ended."

She shrugged. "What choice did you have? You had a child on the way. As you said yourself, you did the right thing."

He had done the right thing. He'd never doubted that. But it didn't mean it had been an easy decision.

"I had no choice," he told her. "I wanted to keep in touch. At the same time I didn't want to hear about you meeting other guys."

She gave him an incredulous look. "Says the man who was married to another woman."

"You know it wasn't like that. Alicia and I...we never fit. We were strangers, really. We married for all the wrong reasons."

"Maybe for all the right reasons." She gave him a sad smile, and he appreciated it, more than she knew.

"You didn't turn your back on your child, and as someone who had a mother who did just that, I can only respect you for your decision." She looked at the sand. "It doesn't mean it was easy, though. It was…so sudden. One minute we were together. The next we couldn't speak to each other again."

"I had to make a clean break. How could it have worked otherwise?" It had torn him up, the loss of what he'd had, a future suddenly full of unknowns.

"It made it easier to go away," she said thoughtfully. "Made it easier to leave Oyster Bay. But looking back, I probably shouldn't have gone to California at all."

He frowned. He'd always wondered if she'd finally found what she was looking for. A meaningful relationship with the mother she'd barely known. A connection with her half-sister. "How was it? With…your mother?"

She gave a strange little smile, but there was hurt in her eyes. "Just like you said it would be. I should have listened to you. If we hadn't fought over it…"

Then they might have stayed together. Had a family of their own. Gone on to do all the things they'd said they would do.

But then there would be no Lucy. And that was…unimaginable.

"You can't make someone be a parent," Hannah said

with a shrug.

"No," Dan said, feeling his appetite subside, even though the fries were salty and warm and the drink was cool and creamy. He forced a bite into his mouth, tasting nothing. "Alicia hasn't reached out to Lucy in over six months. Hasn't seen her in over a year. I blame myself."

"Don't do that," she said sharply, pulling his attention up from his food. There was fire in her eyes, and hurt too. But more than anything, there was determination. She'd always been a person of strong opinions. "My father did that. It always made me feel worse."

"But I couldn't keep the marriage together. I couldn't make her happy." Maybe it had been doomed from the start. They'd tried to make something from nothing. He hadn't ever loved her, not the way a man should love his wife. And she hadn't loved him. "I did the best I could. It wasn't enough. She met someone else."

"Sometimes it doesn't last," Hannah said. "But being a mother and being a wife are two different things. She made her choice. Don't take responsibility for it."

"You ever tell your dad that?" he asked, and Hannah looked away, out onto the ocean and the waves that lapped at the sand.

"There's a lot I need to say to my dad. I just haven't found the right time."

"Bit of advice?" he said, even though he wasn't sure he was the person who could give it anymore. Still, she looked at him earnestly. She seemed lost, somehow, uncertain. "Make the time. You never know when that time is up."

"Life does have a way of throwing curve balls," she said, nodding. She looked down at her food wrappers, and said, "I should probably go. Work day tomorrow and all that."

"You liking your job?" he asked, and Hannah hesitated.

"It's not like the job I had before. It's not my dream job."

"Sometimes that's okay," he said with a grin. She'd always reached for the stars, and he'd loved that about her.

"But I failed," she said, shaking her head. "I went for something, and I couldn't make it last."

He let out a long sigh. "I understand." He shrugged, knowing there wasn't much he could say that would console her. "You tried. At least you have that. And is there anything you would have done differently?"

She thought about this for a bit. "Probably not. But that doesn't mean I didn't mess up somehow."

"It just means that you're ready for a new path," he said. At least he hoped that's what it meant. And a part of him even believed it.

"I had a nice time tonight," he said, as they made their way back into town, where he'd left the car.

"I did too," she said, offering a little smile.

"It's nice. Spending time together." He stopped at the end of the wooden stairs that led them back up to the street. The sun was low in the sky and the lights were starting to come on in the buildings behind her.

She was so pretty. Still so pretty. And sweet. And before he had time to think about what he was doing, he leaned in.

"It's late," she said, taking a step back from him.

He shoved his hands in his pockets, telling himself that she had just spared them both a big mistake. Only, as he followed her up the stairs and they walked back toward the car, he wasn't so sure that was the case anymore.

*

Evie was lying in bed, trying to read a book even though she hadn't absorbed a single word in the past hour, when she saw the headlights of a car through her open window. Curious, she pushed back the thin pink cotton sheet that had been covering her legs, and walked over to the window, careful to position herself behind her curtains.

It was Dan's truck, and Hannah was emerging from the passenger side. She gave barely more than a wave before she all but ran toward the house. There was a rustling at the hedge. A figure that looked like Bev darted in the dark. A moment later, Evie heard the kitchen door close and Hannah's footsteps on the stairs.

Maybe it was because she was bored, or maybe it was because she was just bursting to have someone to share her news with, but she pushed aside all the hurt and rejection that she had felt from her sister and flung open her door just as Hannah reached the top step.

"Out with Dan?"

Hannah's shoulders seemed to roll on her sigh. "It's not how it looks. We went out to dinner. As friends."

Hannah's eyes shifted to the left. A telltale sign that she was lying.

"It's okay to still have feelings for him," Evie said. It was always important to encourage honesty with one's own emotions. She recognized the irony in that immediately. After all, she wasn't exactly being honest with herself about her feelings for Liam, was she?

And was that what it was? Feelings? Or attraction? She didn't know. She didn't recognize herself anymore. Evie the therapist would have been shocked, simply shocked, at such reckless behavior. But Evie the bartender was having fun, not planning for the future, not weighing every decision, the good against the bad, not even thinking about consequences.

From the looks of it, her sister wasn't thinking about consequences either.

"No," Hannah said. "It's not. Dan went his way, and I went mine."

"But now you're both single," Evie pointed out. "You could have a second chance."

"Are you seriously telling me that you believe in all that nonsense?" Hannah looked incredulous as she flicked on her bedroom light and went inside.

Their father was still at the restaurant, and he wouldn't

be home for another hour by Evie's calculation. She followed her sister into her bedroom, uninvited, realizing that she hadn't been in here since Hannah had first left home. The entire room was a time warp, much like her own, bringing her immediately back to a time and place that filled her with comfort and peace and fondness.

Those were good days, even if she and Evie had always been like oil and water. When they were younger, they'd take turns having sleepovers in each other's bedrooms, each taking the role of hostess quite seriously. Evie provided cookies for a bedtime snack on her weeks, and Hannah allowed Evie to cuddle with her favorite brown teddy bear when it was her turn. On rainy afternoons, they'd set up a tent in the attic, playing board games and telling stories and talking about who knew what. Nonsense. By the time they were teenagers, they'd developed separate interests, their personalities driving them apart, but underneath it all, they were still close. They still had each other's backs.

Until Hannah left to find their mother. And their other sister.

Now Evie walked over to the window seat in Hannah's room and lifted the lid. Sure enough, that brown stuffed bear looked back at her, and she smiled, daring to touch it for one quick moment before she shut the seat again and dropped onto it.

"Believe it or not, I had a boyfriend in college," she announced, a little defensively. Sure, her relationship with him was, well, brotherly in a way. Certainly there wasn't any passion, other than their mutual enthusiasm for their studies. But there weren't any butterflies. Or fantasies. Or lust.

All the things that she felt when she saw Liam. The difference was that Liam was fleeting. And passion faded. And that was why Liam was all wrong for her.

Besides, she was not a girl who made decisions with her heart. She made them with her head. After very careful consideration.

"Oh yeah? What happened to him?" Hannah pulled a nightshirt out of her drawer and stepped into her closet.

What had happened to him? Oh, that's right. He said they'd be better off as friends, and she'd agreed. No tears. No sadness. They still kept in touch occasionally.

"We drifted apart. No hard feelings." She shrugged.

Hannah didn't look convinced when she emerged a moment later. "Everyone drifts apart eventually. Or circumstances drive them apart. You'd have to be a fool to think otherwise."

"What about Margo and Eddie? They dated in high school and now they're married, after going their separate ways for years."

"That's one example," Hannah said.

"Abby and Zach," Evie said. It wasn't that she believed it per se herself, but the facts were the facts.

"Oh, Evie," Hannah sighed. "You wouldn't understand."

"Excuse me?" Evie couldn't help it. She felt injured. "I

happen to be a licensed therapist. I'm quite understanding."

"But you've never been in love," Hannah said. "And you've never had your heart broken."

This was true, yes, but she was human, and she did understand feelings. Even if her own were muddled at the moment.

"I'm not that out of touch, Hannah. Believe it or not, I do know a thing or two about relationships."

"Through books?" Hannah shook her head. "I know you don't get out and date, and that's fine, Evie, it's not your thing."

Evie stared at her sister, trying not to say something she would later regret. Was it so hard to believe that she might actually have a romantic life of her own?

Maybe so, and just as well, she thought, as she walked back to her own room and flicked off the bedside light. She was perfectly happy keeping this her little secret. One of many, it would seem.

Chapter Thirteen

By Friday afternoon, Hannah had successfully dodged Dan just as much as she had avoided making eye contact with Bev Wright through the peephole that was permanently carved in the hedge separating their two yards.

She stopped by the *Gazette* to upload her photos for the weekend edition, deciding that a successful first week on the job called for celebration.

"Do you get a lunch break?" she asked Sarah, the office assistant who was right about her age.

Sarah looked up from painting her nails at her desk and grinned. "I was actually just leaving to meet Abby for lunch. I think Melanie's coming too. Want to join?"

A chance to spend time with her cousin Abby was always welcome, and Hannah happily joined Sarah on the walk to Jojo's, another institution that had been around for as long as Hannah could remember.

Melanie and Abby were already outside at one of the pink café tables when Sarah and Hannah arrived, a pitcher of lemonade in front of them.

"Doesn't anyone work in this town?" Hannah joked as she took a seat.

"It's summertime in Oyster Bay," Melanie sighed. "Actually, it's our busy season, if you don't count spring."

"We don't move quite as fast as you did back in San Francisco," Abby said to Hannah, pouring two glasses for the late arrivals.

Hannah was happy for an excuse to take a sip of the drink. She didn't like to think about California, her time there, or even her career at the magazine. She'd slowed her pace the past year, travelling, collecting her thoughts, making a plan, hardening her heart.

She thought back to her conversation with Dan the other night. So much for that. He'd kissed her. And she'd liked it. Liked it so much that she'd replayed it over and over and over.

Yep, another reason to stay away. She couldn't make that mistake twice.

"I need to stop by the inn again soon for another one of your brunches, Abby," she said, still marveling over the fact that Abby had settled down, and not just in the romantic sense. Abby had always flitted from one job to the next, taking life in stride. But she'd found her passion, and as someone with a strong interest of her own,

Hannah admired her for it.

"So Bridget really didn't want to close the inn and go on a honeymoon?" Sarah marveled. Though Hannah didn't know her very well, it was clear that Sarah had strong romantic notions, of the traditional sense. Hannah idly wondered how the prospects were in this town. Other than Timmy, that was.

"They'll go in the fall, she said. But I'm sure business will delay that. I offered to watch the inn for her. And Emma. But, well, you know Bridget." Abby looked a little injured as she picked up her menu and closed it again.

It was inevitable, she supposed. The strain of sisterhood couldn't be escaped. Like herself and Evie, Abby and Bridget were wildly different personalities, but then, they had Margo as a buffer to help balance things out.

Hannah's mind drifted to her other sister, Kelly. She wondered, as she had many times over the years, where their youngest sister would fit into the dynamic, and how things might have been if they'd known each other growing up.

She still hadn't replied to Kelly's email. Just more to feel guilty about, she thought. It wasn't that she wouldn't reply. She just wanted to reply without all these muddled thoughts and conflicted loyalty.

Hannah startled as the waiter approached, and realized that she hadn't even glanced at the menu. "I'll have a Caesar salad," she said. An old staple.

"He was pretty cute," Abby said, looking at Sarah and Melanie.

"And about ten years too young," Melanie said crossly. "Besides, I don't want to be matched up."

"Well, I like being matched up," Sarah said wistfully. "But I have to agree. Abby, that boy was way too young."

"What can I say? Pickings are slim in Oyster Bay." Abby shrugged.

Sarah looked morosely at the lemonade that was causing her glass to sweat. "There was a very handsome man at the singles table at the wedding. But he seemed to only be interested in your other cousin."

"My other cousin?" Abby frowned, then looked over at Hannah. "You mean Evie?"

Hannah almost laughed out loud. Evie wasn't one to flirt with a guy at a wedding. She was much more comfortable sitting by herself in a corner, nursing a glass of ice water. "It couldn't have been Evie."

"It was Evie," Melanie confirmed, and Hannah felt her jaw slack. "And the man was quite handsome."

Abby looked so pleased that her eyes shone. "Well, I'll be. If that doesn't just prove that there's someone for everyone."

"This doesn't make any sense," Hannah said, frowning. "She never said anything to me."

She grew silent, suddenly realizing the harsh truth in that statement. Of course Evie wouldn't have said anything to her. They weren't close like that, and hadn't been for years.

For a while, it hadn't bothered her. It was just how it was. She'd learned not to fight the obvious. She'd seen where that had gotten her with her mother.

But now, being back here, under the same roof, she felt shame. The same shame she felt about her father. Her younger sister had an entire life that she didn't know about. And suddenly, she yearned to be a part of it.

She should have called Evie today, thought to invite her to lunch. Instead she was with her cousin and two friends, and Evie had been cut out of the mix.

She'd change that, she decided. Today. She'd stop by The Lantern before she headed home.

She couldn't deny the ulterior motive that it was an excuse to delay herself, avoid Dan until next week. Her heart sped up every time she thought of the kiss. Whatever it meant, it had happened. And it couldn't happen again.

*

Evie eyed the lobster-shaped clock that had hung above the front entrance of the restaurant. Her stomach did a little dance when she realized she had only had thirty minutes left on her shift. And then...

No reading in bed tonight! Nope, tonight Evie had another date. With Liam. Liam who was strangely mysterious about his past, choosing instead to keep the conversation casual and quick-witted. And Evie, being a bartender these days and not a therapist, decided to just go with this. Who needed an interrogation? Who needed serious heart to hearts? It was summer. She was single. And she was having fun.

Fun! She nearly laughed out loud at the concept. Since when did she have any fun? There was no room for fun, not when she was focused on her goal. There was reading and papers to write and more reading, and more studying.

And now, at the age of twenty-seven, she was finally able to step back and do all the things everyone else around her had been doing while she was sitting in a dim corner of the library until closing.

"I made a big mistake last night, Evie," Ron said as he strolled into the bar. His face was sunburned and he had a wild look in his eyes, and Evie didn't even have to pry to guess what had happened. "I called her."

Huh. Well, that wasn't so bad. Certainly a tamer behavior that punching someone in the nose.

"I called her fifty-six times," he elaborated, and despite all her clinical practice, Evie felt her eyes widen. He gestured to the bar. "Give me a cold one. I need it today."

Evie sighed and turned to fill a glass from the middle tap. Ron liked it poured to the rim, no foam, and she did the best she could to oblige. It was the least she could do, considering the day the man was having.

"Did she answer?" Evie asked as she slid the beer across the bar.

"Of course not," he replied, shaking his head. "Why do you think I called fifty-six times?"

True. Still, she wouldn't put it past him. "What made

you give up?"

"Give up?" He snorted as his eyes filled with tears. "She turned off her phone."

Of course she had, Evie wanted to say, but she refrained. Sometimes, just being a compassionate listener was all the patient needed. Sometimes, they worked things out for themselves. Sometimes they had no one else to talk to. Sometimes they didn't need advice.

And in Ron's case, they wouldn't be inclined to take it.

Still, when he gave a hard sniff and looked up at her and asked what the hell he should do next, she knew it was time to speak up. "I think that you should focus on yourself a bit. What are some of things you enjoyed doing before you met Jill?"

He blinked a few times. "Jeez. I don't even remember back that far."

"Okay, then, what is something you enjoy doing? Other than tracking down Jill, calling her, or thinking about her."

He gave a sly smile. "Does stalking her Facebook account count?"

She knew she shouldn't, but she smiled, even if she did manage to pinch her mouth by the end.

"The next time I see you, I want a list of five things you enjoy doing that have absolutely no connection to your wife, okay?"

He seemed to mull this over for a moment. "Okay. I can do that."

"You said that on Sunday and I haven't seen the list. This is your homework before our next session. I mean, meeting," she quickly corrected herself. Jesus.

"Homework. Yes, ma'am!" Ron gave a little smile as he sipped his beer.

Good. She felt a swell of pride in her chest. She was helping him. And damn if that didn't feel good.

The afternoon was waning, and the bar was filling quickly. She mixed three margaritas for some tourists from Philly, and a Long Island Iced Tea for Cassie at the end of the bar, who was slowly recovering from the sudden break up and starting to enjoy the distraction of a change of scenery for the week. Evie didn't even need to consult her mixing guide anymore, she realized, not that this was something to exactly brag about.

She added a bag of ice to the cooler and looked up to see Hannah sitting next to Cassie. Her smile was friendly, but Evie was suspicious.

"Dad's in the back," she offered, as she scooped ice into a glass.

"Actually I came by to see you. What time does your shift end?"

Evie looked at the clock, her stomach fluttering when she noted the time. "Ten minutes." In ten minutes she would walk out the door, and toward the beach, where Liam would be waiting with a bottle of wine and a hamper of ready-to-go food from The Corner Market, as promised.

"Want to grab dinner tonight? I haven't been to

Dunley's in forever," Hannah said.

Evie refrained from pointing out that this was because Hannah had not been home in forever.

"I have plans tonight." She turned to fill a beer from the tap for Bill down at the end of the bar, who had been unemployed for two years and was only now starting to panic, knowing that she should offer up something in exchange, like dinner another night, or a nightcap when she got home. If she wanted to self-analyze, she might say that she was punishing her sister. Being passive aggressive, even. She was human, after all.

"Oh yeah? What are you up to?" Hannah asked.

Maybe she was just being conversational, or maybe she couldn't believe that Evie the book nerd could actually have plans on a Friday night, but either way, Evie didn't feel like sharing. Sharing would mean explaining, and just as her sister had accused the other night, this time the tables were turned: Hannah wouldn't understand.

Or maybe Hannah wouldn't even believe her.

Either way, telling Hannah, or anyone for that matter, would ruin this special, fluttery, half-nauseous feeling she had every morning when she woke up and every evening when she left Liam's company.

And she didn't mind holding onto it. For a little while at least.

Chapter Fourteen

Hannah spent all of Saturday morning sitting on a faded beach chair with a book that didn't catch her interest and a camera that was now full of sunrises, sunsets, the occasional candid of a passerby.

Evie had gone into town, presumably to take a shift at the restaurant, but Hannah wasn't so sure this was the case. Her sister was being decidedly evasive, and after what Abby and the girls had said, she was starting to wonder just what she was hiding.

With a yawn, she stood up and stretched. The sand was between her toes and no doubt in her hair, but she didn't mind. She'd grown up like this. Long days at the beach, late nights getting in. The outdoor shower stall behind the garage had been their summer bath.

Sometimes, she was sure she even wore the same sundress for days on end, but she didn't care. Chip made sure to cover what really mattered: teeth were always clean and hair was always washed, even if it wasn't always brushed. They had to wash their hands before every meal, and they always had to mind their manners. They'd grown independent at a young age. Hannah remembered the time she was sick from sneaking too many strawberries from the pints Chip brought home from the farmers market. He was at the table, paying bills, and Evie was outside jumping rope. Hannah was on the old tire swing that still hung from the old elm, and the more it swayed, the more her stomach turned, until she had to dash to the bushes and come out wiping her mouth, her eyes tearing.

Evie was oblivious, being only about four at the time, and Hannah knew that she could either bother her father, or just deal with things herself. She'd rinsed her mouth from the hose in the lawn, then gone inside, brushed her teeth, put on her favorite nightgown, and climbed into bed. No big deal.

Her father was working hard to provide for them. He never complained, and she knew he would have dropped everything to take care of her. He probably would have put a cold washcloth on her forehead and everything, the way he'd done the winter before when Evie had come down with a fever.

But it wasn't her father that Hannah wanted in that moment. It was her mother. Only her mother was gone, her sole communication had been a few random letters and the occasional birthday present. The last one being a dress that was two sizes too small, and had instead gone to Evie.

Hannah walked back to the house now, taking care not to make eye contact with the Wrights' house as she passed by it. She walked around to the back of their property, past the tire swing, past the garden hose, and pulled her old bike free from the back of the garage. The tires needed air, but they'd be fine to get her into town quicker than her tired legs would, and she needed the escape.

She pedaled hard, up over the bluff, taking the long way into town to enjoy the scenery, stopping occasionally to snap a shot when inspiration struck. By the time she hit Main Street, beads of sweat had collected at the back of her neck, and she parked her bike in front of the ice cream parlor, hoping they still made those delicious frozen pink lemonades she'd been so crazy about as a kid. Back then she and Abby would go into town together, on one bike, sharing the seat just as they had the other day. The deal was that one would pedal into town and the other would pedal back, that way they each got a rest. Of course, it was always better to pedal into town, so you could rest on the return journey, but they'd never argued. They'd alternated.

Where was Evie on all those trips? Hannah frowned, thinking that Evie must have been too young to go into town on her own, and of course the bike seat could only fit two, and barely.

Evie was probably curled up on her window seat in her bedroom, reading a book or writing in her journal, perfectly content. Still, Hannah had a sudden wish to go back in time, knock on her little sister's door, invite her along.

She walked up to the outside window of the ice cream parlor and ordered a frozen pink lemonade, large. She couldn't help smiling when it was handed to her, and boy did it go down quickly. She paused, telling herself to slow down before she did something even more childish and gave herself a brain freeze, and walked around to the side of the shop to find a table in the shade.

And there he was. Or rather, there they were. Dan and his daughter, licking cones, totally relaxed. Their simple companionship spoke more than a hundred words. This was Dan's life now. His family. His comfort. This was the person he could sit in silence with, feeling completely at peace.

Once, it had been her.

It would be too obvious to turn and run now, so she managed a smile and, catching Dan's look of surprise, said, "Hello."

"Hey!" He quickly leaned forward in his chair, seeming startled at her presence.

Hannah was reminded in that moment that she was technically an outsider, and she'd yet again interrupted a family moment.

"Hello again, Lucy," she said. She looked at Dan. "I didn't mean to interrupt."

"You can sit with us if you'd like," Lucy said, smiling at her.

Hannah hesitated. This wasn't her place. This was Dan's family. Dan's life. And she wasn't a part of it. Never had been.

"I don't want to intrude," she said, shifting the weight on her feet uneasily.

"You're not intruding," Dan said with a smile. Without another word, he slid the extra chair back from the table and patted it.

"Do you come here a lot?" Hannah asked as she took her seat. She wasn't used to being around children, but she did have a younger sister, two in fact, and she'd been a little girl herself once.

"Sometimes. I like coming here with my friends. When my dad lets me." Lucy gave Dan a stern look that made Hannah smile. She was keeping him on his toes, and she was starting to like this feisty child.

"She's mad that I'm making her wait until she's twelve until she can ride her bike into town on her own," Dan explained with a rueful smile.

"Ah." Hannah nodded. Oyster Bay wasn't exactly filled with crime, not unless you counted things like penny candy being stolen from The Corner Market, but things happened, kids got hurt. People too, but not in the physical sense.

She paused for a moment to realize the irony of this

situation. Ten years ago, did she ever think she would be sitting here, with Dan and his daughter from his ex-wife, enjoying a Sunday afternoon with ice cream and frozen lemonade?

She almost laughed out loud.

"Da-ad!" Lucy dragged out the word and gave him a fake punch, but even though her mouth was pinched, there was a smile in her eyes.

"You'll understand some day," was all Dan said, and Hannah marveled at the truth in such a common statement. Hindsight was always clearer. The twisted thing about it was that it was too late to go back and change anything.

"What are you up to today?" Dan asked.

Hannah shrugged, feeling put on the spot. Taking photos seemed like the obvious, if not overused, response, and she tried to think of something else, some purpose to her weekend. Maybe she would go visit Margo or Abby.

"I—" But before she had a chance to think of an excuse, Beverly Wright sauntered over, a gleam in her gaze and a determination in her walk.

"Oh, how nice to see you all together," Bev said, her eyes taking the three of them in. "So, I guess things are going well, from what I see!"

"Just enjoying an afternoon ice cream, Bev," Dan said diplomatically.

"Enjoying more than that, no doubt!" Bev said. She

glanced at Hannah, perhaps hoping that Hannah would elaborate, but Hannah just smiled sweetly and took another sip from her lemonade.

"And what are your plans for the rest of the day?" Bev asked pertly.

Hannah blinked. She was just as unsure how to answer Bev's question as she'd been to answer Dan's. She had considered going home, relaxing on the hammock, but no doubt Bev would be peeping through the hole she'd cut in the hedge, and assuming all sorts of things. And would she send Timmy over? Likely.

"It's spaghetti night," Lucy informed her. "We always have Spaghetti Saturdays!"

"What a sweet tradition," Bev said, putting a hand to her heart. "It's nice that you...keep those up," she said to Dan, whose jaw seemed to tense. Perhaps catching the change in mood, she announced, "Well, I'm off. Timmy has a date tonight. A nice young lady he met at the wedding, and I need to help him get ready."

Hannah felt her eyes widen and she didn't dare look in Dan's direction.

Bev seemed to waver, as if hoping she had called Hannah's bluff. Finally, with her shoulders slumping in defeat, she said, "I don't want to interrupt your...together time. But I'm happy for you, Dan. Very, very, very happy." With one last glance in Hannah's direction, Bev marched away, her sigh of disappointment audible.

Hannah and Dan exchanged a long sigh across the table. "You owe me," Dan said.

"Owe you?" Hannah laughed.

"I saved you," Dan said with a knowing grin.

Hannah sighed and sipped her lemonade. "I suppose you did, in a way. But you owed me," she said, before she could stop herself. Hurt had a way of creeping in just when she was starting to let her guard down.

Dan's smile faded, and he looked at her pensively, sadly.

Eager to change the subject, Hannah turned to Lucy. "So, Spaghetti Saturdays, huh?"

"Come for dinner tonight!" Lucy suggested.

Hannah felt her face heat immediately, and she started shaking her head, trying to think of an excuse. This was their weekly tradition. Their family tradition. Not her place.

"Yes," Dan said, before she could object. "Come for dinner tonight."

Hannah looked from Dan into the matching eyes of his sweet little girl, seeing something in them that resonated deep. Something of herself, maybe.

And how could she say no?

*

Dan lived in the same house he had grown up in, on the edge of town, at the end of Creek Lane. She'd been to the house at least a hundred times, but it had changed since then. Now it was no longer Mr. and Mrs. Fletcher's house. Now it was Dan's house, where he lived as a father, where he'd lived as a husband.

She swept her eyes around the hall as Lucy greeted her at the screen door. The paint on the outside of the house was fresh, and the furniture was different, but it still felt more like Dan than, well...the woman he'd lived with for nearly a decade.

"I brought some berries for dessert," Hannah said, handing the pint to Lucy, who accepted them with a smile. "I wasn't sure you were allowed ice cream twice in one day."

"In the summer I am allowed ice cream twice in one day," Lucy said earnestly.

Hannah grinned and pulled an angel food cake and a pint of fresh raspberry ice cream from her tote. "Good!"

Lucy giggled as she struggled to carry all the items and hurried them back to the kitchen, not bothering to show Hannah the way, even though Hannah already knew this house by heart. She took her time, opting to leave on her sandals when she spotted Dan through the back window, sitting on the deck. She glanced at a wall of photos, taking stock. Lucy at all stages of life. Dan, looking so young, just the way she'd last seen him, holding her wrapped in a pale pink blanket. If there were any photos of Lucy's mother in the house, they must have been somewhere else.

She thought of Lucy, that smile and those shining eyes. She hoped there was a photo of her mother in this house. She hoped there were many.

Her own father had always kept them out, until

enough time had gone by that Hannah had objected, tears streaming down her face as she shattered one of the frames to the ground. Chip had said nothing, just silently watched, the distress in his face evident as he quietly bent to pick up the pieces. "I'm sorry, sweetheart," she'd heard him say as she'd run outside to the swing.

But what was he sorry about, she'd thought at the time. Now she knew, of course. Now she saw it all so much differently.

Oh, Dad, she thought, feeling that tug in her chest again.

Dan was opening the back door now, grinning at her as she entered the kitchen. "I didn't know you'd arrived or I would have greeted you."

"It's okay," she said. "I know my way."

He nodded slowly, jamming his hands into his pockets. "It's changed a bit."

"It has," she agreed. But not so much. Still, she felt weird and out of place being here. She jutted her chin to the back deck. She'd be much more comfortable outside. "It's a nice night."

"It is," he said, opening the door. "If it were up to me, I would have grilled burgers, but...traditions and all."

She blinked in surprise, thinking of Dan having family traditions, setting them, following them, honoring them. "You're a real adult," she marveled as he opened the door for her to pass.

He cocked an eyebrow. "And you're not?"

"Doesn't feel like it most of the time," she sighed.

There was a bottle of wine on the table, chilling in a bucket of ice, and a pitcher of iced tea, too. She opted for the tea, sitting down as Dan poured. Lucy had disappeared into the house, but Hannah assumed she'd be back soon. Her own glass of lemonade was half full and the ice was quickly melting.

"Sometimes I feel like I'm just bumbling through life," she elaborated. The trip to South America had been proof of that.

"Don't we all?" Dan surprised her by saying. "Sometimes I wake up and I think, I have a child, who isn't so little any more, and I still don't know what the hell I'm doing half the time. But she thinks I do. How's that for strange?" He cocked an eyebrow again, making her smile, like they were in on something together, some secret admission that they didn't reveal to anyone else.

"I shouldn't have gone to California," she blurted. "I never should have planned it to begin with. If I hadn't..." She stopped. There was no point in finishing that thought. Woulda, coulda, shouldas. Would it have ended any differently? Maybe she and Dan would have stayed together? But for how long? It hadn't taken much to drive them apart in the first place.

"What was it like?" Dan asked carefully.

"Oh." Hannah leaned back in her chair and blew out a breath. "Disappointing. I don't know what I could have expected. My mother was just as disinterested in me as she'd ever been. My other sister, Kelly...I'm glad we bonded. But that causes problems with Evie. And then there's my dad. I know I hurt him by going."

Dan was silent for moment. "Sometimes I wonder how I'll feel if Lucy goes after Alicia someday. It's just been the two of us for so long. A part of me doesn't think that her mother deserves her. At the same time, I know that Lucy probably needs her. And I want that for her."

Hannah chewed her lip, wondering if this is how her own father felt. There was only one way to find out, if she finally worked up the courage to discuss it with him.

"I never thought I would be a good mother," she admitted.

Dan frowned. "Why would you say that?"

Hannah shrugged, trying to keep her voice casual, but something in her was breaking. "Because I never had one of my own? I don't know what a mother and daughter relationship is even supposed to be. I mean, I've seen it, from the outside, but day to day...I wouldn't know what to do."

Dan was quiet for a long time. "A girl needs a mother. That's what the busybodies in town always tell me. As if it were somehow my fault that Alicia walked out on us."

"Oh, I don't think they're blaming you," Hannah said.

"Blaming me for not moving on," Dan said. He gave her a small smile. "It's been nice, these past couple weeks. Having them off my back."

"Happy to be at your service," Hannah said, realizing that it was true. Dan was struggling, as a father, as a man who wanted to give his daughter everything but could only give her what was within his control. If she could make that a little easier on him, it felt good.

"For what it's worth," she said, "I think you're doing fine on your own."

"I try," Dan said. "You learn as you go. Parenting doesn't come with a manual. You'd be fine at it."

"Yeah?" She studied him, not convinced. His gaze was steady, his face free of all amusement.

"Yeah," he said. "You'd...be a really good mother. I probably shouldn't say this, but for a long time, I used to think, what it might have been like, if..."

She held up a hand. She didn't want to hear this. "There are no ifs," she said firmly. "There's just the facts."

He nodded. "I know. But it didn't stop me from thinking about what might have been."

She looked down. She hadn't thought he'd thought of her in all these years. She'd just assumed that she was forgotten, replaced by his instant family, by the life he'd chosen.

"I tried to make the best of it," he said. "But a part of me..." He trailed off and shook his head. "Well, like you said, no point talking in hyoptheticals."

"Nope," she said firmly. It just messed with your heart. Made you long for things that hadn't been and couldn't be.

The back door opened with a bang and Lucy stood impatiently. "Dad! Time to make the spaghetti!"

Dan cocked an eyebrow in invitation, and Hannah laughed. She wasn't much of a cook, but then, today was full of new experiences. She grinned back at him. "Why not?"

*

Dan looked down at the empty plates on the table. It was the best Spaghetti Saturday they'd had in a while, and not just because the food had come out better than usual. Lucy had giggled and smiled the entire time, in a way he'd almost forgotten she could. Sure she smiled, still laughed, and had her moments at the beach, but tonight...tonight it was laughter right from the belly. Smiles right from the heart.

"I forgot," Hannah said abruptly. She opened her bag that was resting at her feet and pulled out an envelope.

Dan took it, confused, and slowly peeled back the flap. Inside was a photo of him and Lucy, taken at the beach. He stared at it for a long time, and finally looked up at Hannah. "This is a real gift. I don't have enough of these."

"It's nothing," she said.

"It's a lot," he said, staring at the photo, squinting a bit as night encroached. "Lucy looks so happy."

"She is happy," Hannah said. "The camera doesn't lie."

He'd like to believe that. And looking at this photo, he almost could.

"Just so you know," Dan said, leaning across the table to Hannah and lowering his voice so Lucy wouldn't wake up and hear them through her partially open window. "I think you really made Lucy's night."

Hannah gave a modest smile, but he could see she was pleased. "Raspberry ice cream has a way of working with little girls. I know from experience."

"You had her laughing…" Dan shook his head. "I haven't heard that laugh in too long."

A look passed between them. Sympathy, perhaps. "Something tells me she'll be giggling about Abby giving me a ride on her bike for a week. Or she'll be begging you for a bike with a banana seat."

"As I said, you made her night," Dan said. He looked at her. "You made mine too."

Hannah hesitated. "Danny."

He shook his head. "You don't need to say anything. I just want to thank you. It meant a lot."

Hannah reached over and set her hand on his. It was felt warm and smooth and so terribly familiar. "She adores you."

"I know," he said, grinning, and she grinned back, swatting his hand away, which filled him with regret.

"You always were a cocky one," she said ruefully.

"Ah, but you liked that about me," he pointed out.

"I did," she admitted. "But this other side of you is nice, too. This…family side. It suits you."

"It suits you, too," he said, realizing just how true this way. With Hannah here tonight, everything had clicked into place. He'd never had a Spaghetti Saturday with Alicia. It was something he'd invented after she left, to give Lucy something to look forward to, to rely on. Just the two of them.

Only tonight it had been three. A third person who had joined in the fun, told them stories and made them laugh, brought the house to life with warmth. It had never been that way before, when Alicia was living here. He'd done his best, and they'd both loved Lucy in their own ways, but there was no family unit. Alicia did her thing, and he did his. When they were together, they argued.

It hadn't just been Hannah he had missed all these years. It was this: this happiness, this togetherness, this comfort of connection and understanding.

"I should help clean up," Hannah said, sliding her chair back from the deck.

Dan stood, but set a hand on her wrist when she reached for a plate. She looked up at him, her eyes widening in surprise, and he leaned in, slowly this time, his heart gaining speed as their lips touched and he kissed her, properly, for real, just like he had a hundred times before, yet never like tonight.

"That was nice," he said, when she pulled away. "All of it."

She nodded. "It was."

"Maybe we can do this again. If you're up for it."

Hannah paused long enough for him to wonder if he'd

gone too far, overstepped. But then she gave a little smile. "I'd like that."

Me too, he thought. Me too.

Chapter Fifteen

Dan woke up the next morning to the sound of pots clanging in the kitchen. He frowned, wondering if he'd somehow lost track of the days. But no, it was most definitely Sunday, and Mrs. Quinn never worked Sundays.

He threw back the covers and stumbled downstairs, following the smell of burning toast and Lucy's chatter, going through a mental rolodex of who could have come over, and who Lucy might have let in the house. She knew never to open the door to strangers.

He hurried down the hall, wondering for one fleeting, wonderful moment if Hannah had stopped by, or if Mrs. Quinn had picked something up for them at the market and brought it by early, but when he saw the woman in the kitchen, he stopped, and it felt for one moment as if the world had tilted, the way it had when Alicia had told him she was pregnant, and the way it had when she told him she was leaving.

"You're back." It came out as more of an accusation than a question, as intended. But maybe it should be an accusation. She'd disappeared, barely kept in touch, and now she had just waltzed back into their lives, as casually as if she'd just run to the store. Had she even knocked?

Lucy turned and smiled at him, showing nearly all her teeth, her grin was so broad. His heart sank at the light in her eyes, at the joy and hope and elation that filled them. Oh, honey, he thought. It's just not that easy.

Alicia's expression was considerably more sober when she turned to face him. "Hello, Dan."

He didn't even realize he was clenching his teeth until his jaw began to ache. He rubbed it, calculating what to do next, careful with Lucy present. Since Alicia had left, they'd never spoken. Paperwork had been filed, by her, sent through an attorney located in Philadelphia. That was the most he knew of her whereabouts, other than the return address labels that came on the few cards or gifts she'd sent Lucy. When she called, he made sure Lucy answered. The way he saw it, she'd made her choice. She'd moved out. He'd moved on.

But now?

"I didn't hear you come in," he said, venturing farther into the room. Still, he kept a distance. She was being overly familiar. Presumptuous, really. And he was tired of her calling the shots at his toll.

Her smile was only slightly apologetic. "I drove all

night. I got here so early that I used the key under that clay frog in the backyard and let myself in. I didn't want to wake you," she added.

He nodded. This wasn't her house anymore. Maybe it had never been her house. It was his childhood home, and now it was his and Lucy's home. Maybe Alicia had always sensed that. Maybe they should never have lived here. Maybe, maybe, maybe.

He glanced at Lucy, who was happily offering him a plate of extremely burnt toast. "We made breakfast!"

"I see that," he said. He looked back at Alicia, trying to hide the mix of emotions that were rolling through him. They'd finally come to a good place. They'd adjusted. Made it work. And now their lives were turned upside down again. Change after change, dictated by Alicia, with Dan left to scramble to react and pick up the pieces. "After breakfast we should talk."

"Mommy's going to take me shopping in town after breakfast!" Lucy announced excitedly. "We're going to go back to school shopping for all new clothes and then we're going to get our nails done. I'm going to get blue glittery polish. And we're going to have frozen lemonades and everything!"

"You can come." Alicia looked at him, and for a moment a heavy silence fell in the room. She knew he wouldn't come. And part of him didn't even want Lucy to go. Why fill her head with dreams if they would all be shattered by end of day, no doubt?

But much as he wanted to protect his daughter, he also didn't want to take this opportunity from her.

"We can talk when you get back," he said as he turned to go upstairs to shower.

If she was coming back, he thought. And he suddenly wasn't so sure that was best after all.

*

Hannah couldn't fight the smile on her face as she walked down Main Street, her camera swinging against her chest, her tote bag roped over her shoulder, her ponytail positively bouncing. Who was this girl? She'd slept better than she had in months, and woken feeling free and almost hopeful. Her father was gone, already at the restaurant, and Evie was out too, though Hannah wasn't so sure where she was. She supposed she could stop by The Lantern, scope out the situation, but it was getting weird seeing Evie in there, giving out advice to all the day drinkers who came to her with their tears and problems, and half the time Hannah wished she could do the same. Drop down, ask for a generous pour, and tell her just how disappointed she was. Just how lost she felt. Just how much she'd lost and screwed up.

But this morning she didn't feel that way. This morning she felt at peace with her past. Eager to move forward. She was going to talk to her father. Make things right. And then she'd move on to Evie. See if they could grow close again, the way sisters should.

Her mind traveled to her other sister. And then...she'd

reply to Kelly. She missed Kelly. And she couldn't admit that to anyone here. Kelly was sweet and smart and fun, and like herself, Kelly was creative. She had ideas, big ideas, for all sorts of things she wanted to try and do. It wasn't like that with Evie, who saw the world so matter-of-factly. Hannah always felt the need to explain her passion for photography to Evie, who would nod with a vacant look in her eyes that told Hannah she didn't approve, whereas Kelly was eager to hear about her ideas, her projects. It had been Kelly who suggested somewhere along Hannah's year-long trip to South America that she even consider making a project of it. A book, perhaps, or just a gallery showing.

Deep down, Hannah wasn't so sure how well Kelly and Evie would get along. If they ever met...

The day was hot. Hannah dropped onto a bench in the town square and observed her surroundings, lifting her camera to take a few shots of the rose bushes and the elderly couple near the gazebo. It wasn't until she had zoomed in all the way with her lens that she realized it was Mimi and Earl. She frowned, looking at the way Earl held Mimi's hand, and the content smile that filled Mimi's face.

Something in her heart turned a little, well, mushy. And she didn't think it could do that anymore. She lifted her camera again, snapped a few photos, vowing to print and frame them as an anniversary present for those two.

She stood, not wanting to interrupt their time together

before she was spotted, and walked back to the street. And right into Alicia Hudson. Or rather, Alicia Fletcher.

She blinked, trying to process what was happening, not quite believing her own eyes until she looked down and saw Lucy, in a pale yellow sundress and a smile nearly as bright as her eyes.

"Hannah! Hannah! Look! My mommy came back!"

Lucy's grin was so huge and heartfelt, that Hannah felt the backs of her eyes prickle when she looked at the little girl. But the emotion was there for another reason.

She blinked again, this time pushing back tears, trying to recover her shock, trying to hide the horror that she was sure was all over her face, and looked straight at the woman who had spent all those years at Dan's side. And who had chosen to walk away.

And who was back. She was back!

"Hello, Hannah." Alicia managed a brittle smile and then pinched her lips. "I didn't know you were back in town."

"I didn't know you were either," Hannah replied evenly. She saw Alicia's eyebrow lift in acknowledgement.

"I didn't know that you and Lucy knew each other," Alicia said. She frowned a bit, looking down at her daughter for clarification.

There are a lot of things you don't know, Hannah wanted to say, but Lucy was present, clinging to her mother's hand, and so Hannah said nothing. This wasn't her family drama. It wasn't her place to try to save Lucy. Or replace Alicia. Really, it didn't even feel like her place to be standing here at all.

"Hannah came to Spaghetti Saturday!" Lucy was happy to offer.

"Spaghetti Saturday?" Alicia frowned deeper, and then, perhaps remembering she had an audience, rolled back her shoulders and rearranged her expression.

"Every Saturday Dad and I make spaghetti!" Lucy added.

"How…nice." Alicia looked confused, and Hannah realized that she hadn't intruded last night at all. That she hadn't slipped into Alicia's place.

She looked at Lucy, who was still beaming. She could never slip into Alicia's place.

"I only came the one time," Hannah said, wondering why she had bothered. She didn't need to deny or defend her relationship with Dan and Lucy.

Relationship, she thought. There was no relationship. She was a person from his past. And these two people? They were his family.

"Well, we should run. I promised Lucy we'd have a frozen lemonade before we went home."

Home. She still called Dan's house home. And less than twenty-four hours ago, Hannah had been in that home. In Alicia's home.

She backed away, managing a tight smile that felt frozen on her face. "Enjoy your day, Lucy. It was very nice running into you."

"You too!" Lucy said as Alicia led her away.

Hannah stood and watched as Dan's family crossed the street and went to the ice cream parlor. Mother and daughter, hand in hand, as it should be. And Dan, at home, waiting for their safe return.

As it should be.

And nowhere in that equation did Hannah have any place. She never had.

Chapter Sixteen

By eight o'clock that night, Alicia had shown no signs of leaving. Her suitcases were still stacked in the front hall, and Lucy was curled up beside her on the couch, watching a movie they'd selected together.

Dan sat in the armchair, trying to focus on the television screen, but his eyes kept drifting back to Alicia. After she had left, he had hoped for this day, if not for himself, then for Lucy. But now that she was here, the thought of going back to that life, the coldness, the separation, the tension and arguments...it killed him.

His mind was spinning, wondering what the right thing was. Eleven years ago, when Alicia had told him about the baby, it had been clear, black and white, no grey area. He would stand by her. He would be a father. He would leave Hannah and all their plans and hopes and dreams.

But now, after years of trying to make that life work, it hadn't. And Alicia had agreed it hadn't. She'd been the one to quit first.

Everything he'd done had been for Lucy. He would do what was best for her again, he told himself. That would be the right thing to do.

He kissed Lucy goodnight and watched them go upstairs. Heard the murmurs of Alicia tucking their daughter into bed. He stood, folded the blanket on the couch, wandered into the kitchen, contemplated pouring himself a beer, and then deciding to hold off, wait until after the conversation.

Alicia returned a few minutes later. She hovered in the doorway. The distance between them, in every possible way, was obvious.

"I saw Hannah in town," she said, catching him by surprise. "Lucy said that she came to something called a Spaghetti Saturday. How quaint."

"It's not quaint," Dan ground out, rising to the defense of Hannah and his weekly tradition, even though he knew the fact that he had to explain it at all was proof of how far apart he and Alicia had drifted. "It's something Lucy and I do each week. She looks forward to it. On the weekends I'm home more. More time to cook. It helped, having these things to look forward to, after…" He trailed off.

She nodded, quiet for a moment. Finally she tipped her head. "And does Hannah come every time?"

"She came once," Dan said firmly, wondering why he

was bothering to explain. It wasn't her business. She'd left. She'd filed the papers.

"Lucy seems fond of her," Alicia said, her expression unreadable.

Dan knew it was a test. He could keep the peace. Nod. Say nothing. Or he could have the honest conversation that was needed.

"I'm fond of her, too," he said.

Alicia's expressed twitched, but she quickly recovered. "We never should have gotten married, Dan. I think you know that too."

"I just tried to the do the right thing," Dan said.

Alicia nodded. "I know. And I should have seen that. But all the arguments and fights...it overshadowed everything."

"I tried," Dan said, feeling an ache in his chest when he thought of all those unhappy years, the only shining light being Lucy. "I really tried to make it work. For Lucy."

"I know. And I did too. But it caught up with me, I guess." She looked at him across the room. "I resented you."

He nodded. He knew. "I know." It hadn't been the life she'd wanted either. Like him, she'd given up hopes and dreams. And at the end of the day, they had no one to blame but each other.

"I wanted a happy family. For Lucy." He wanted the world for her.

"A child can have a happy family without two parents," Alicia said. "But I want to be a part of her life, Dan. I know I messed up. I know I disappeared. I was just so unhappy, and I was blaming all the wrong people. None of this was your fault. Or her fault. I needed some time, to figure out what I wanted to do with my life. It had been a long time since I'd thought about those things."

He stared at her. Not sure where she was going with this. "I'm going to college. In the fall. I applied at University of Maine and I got accepted."

University of Maine. She was staying in state. But not in Oyster Bay.

"I'd like to be a part of Lucy's life. I always wanted that. I just…I'm sorry."

"Lucy is the one you should apologize to," Dan said flatly. "You can't just come and go as you please. You're her mother."

She nodded, unable to meet his eye. "I know it will take some time to make up for what I did. But I also know that I needed some time away. I think I'll be a better mother now. A happier mother. Don't you want that to?" She looked at him. "To have her look back and remember her parents smiling and happy, not arguing and fighting all the time?"

He pulled in a long breath and let it out slowly. He did want that. It was just awful it had to get to this point.

"How long are you in town for?" he asked.

"Fall session starts next Monday," Alicia said. "I'll

head out Friday night to get settled."

"Through the week," he said. And then his little girl's heart would break all over again. And he'd be left to adjust and change and deal with the fallout.

"I don't have to stay here," Alicia said, but Dan held up a hand.

"You're Lucy's mother. You're always welcome here."

Alicia looked down at the ground, and even though they were still standing a room length apart, Dan felt in that moment that for the first time in all the years they'd known each other that they were finally connected.

"I want you to be happy, Dan," she finally said.

She looked at him, and he closed his eyes briefly against the pain in her gaze, and the honesty. "I want you to be happy too," he said. He smiled, the first smile he had offered her in a long time, he realized.

They were going to be okay. All of them. And with any hope, they would be the best they had ever been.

*

By the middle of the week, Hannah still hadn't heard from Dan. She had left the house at the crack of dawn, camera in hand, taking shots of the sunrise on her way into work, where she was the first person to show up, other than Sarah, who was there with the key to open the door.

She didn't come home until the sun had set, when his truck was gone, when he'd gone back to his house. To his family.

She didn't want to hear his explanations. She didn't want to know what had happened. Lucy's mother was home. All was right. As it should be.

On Wednesday night, she let herself into the kitchen, which was slowly being transformed into something wonderful. Each day she saw the progress. The proof of Dan's presence. She imagined him in the kitchen, installing the cabinets, the fixtures, chipping away at a project, working hard to provide for his child. He was right here, in her house, day after day, and she'd never felt more far away from him.

She opened the fridge, pulled out a yogurt, and jumped when she saw her father standing beside her when she closed the door.

"You scared me," she said, smiling nervously.

"I haven't seen much of you around lately," Chip said. He gave a sheepish smile. "I was starting to wonder if you were avoiding me."

She looked up at him guiltily, and something inside her broke when their eyes met. His soft blue gaze crinkled at the corners, and his smile was kind, as it had always been.

"Oh, Dad." Hannah let out a shaky sigh, and for a moment, she feared she would burst into tears. She didn't want her father to hug her right now. She didn't deserve to be hugged. She needed to apologize to him first. To explain. Everything.

"It was actually Dan I was avoiding, really," she said, and now the tears really prickled the backs of her eyes, and she looked down at the yogurt container, her appetite lost, knowing she wouldn't even open it.

"I didn't know you were coming back to town when I hired him," Chip said. He gave her a little grin. "But would it be so wrong for me to admit that I hoped throwing the two of you together would lead to a little reconciliation?"

"Are you saying that you were hoping to match us up?" Hannah lifted an eyebrow. Since when did her father meddle in things like that?

"I just wanted what was best for you…and I hoped…When I saw the two of you together at the rehearsal dinner and the wedding, I thought…" He shook his head. "I shouldn't have interfered."

"It came from a good place. Besides, Dan and I didn't need your match-making help. We did it all on our own." She followed her father to the table and told him the whole, ridiculous story. "So, it wasn't your plan, Dad. And besides, the plan didn't work."

"I'm sorry, honey. I know how much Dan meant to you once." Her father set a hand on her arm, a simple, small gesture, and it was all it took for the floodgates to open.

"I'm the one who is sorry, Dad. I never should have thought to go out there, chasing after Mom. I messed everything up. Things with Danny. Evie. You." She looked up at him through watery eyes, surprised to see the confusion that creased his forehead.

"You did not mess anything up with me. I understand why you went to California, Hannah."

She wiped away a tear. "You do?"

"Of course!" Chip pulled in a sigh. "All your life I felt bad that you didn't have a mother. When you went out there...Well, I could only hope that you had found what you were looking for."

"I didn't."

Her father tipped his head, his shoulders sagging in defeat. "Oh, honey. I'm so sorry."

"I don't know what I expected. I thought...I hoped..."

"Hope is a good thing," her father said with a smile. "And I'm glad I raised you girls to have it. You went after something. You didn't find it. But you know you are always welcome here. Go out into the world. Search for what you must. But this is always your home, Hannah."

"I don't think Evie feels that way," Hannah said through falling tears.

"Evie is different. She's your sister. She has her own complex feelings about your mother, I'm sure. She's just chosen to handle it differently. She'll come around. It takes her longer to process things sometimes. She's in her head more than you are. You always followed your heart."

Hannah narrowed her eyes to that thought. "Not anymore."

"Look at this," he said, sliding a box to the center of the table and lifting the lid. He pulled out a photo of Evie and Hannah, taken at Christmas, when Evie was just a baby. They wore matching red dresses and bows. They looked like dolls.

"Where did you find this?" she asked, rummaging through the rest of the box. There was one of her mother, sitting on her bed, a book on the table. She looked so young! And...happy. Another of her at her dressing table, getting ready for a night out. There were others, moments she hadn't remembered. But maybe none of them were memories.

"You used to look through these pictures all the time when you were little. Then you got upset that one time and, well, I put them away."

"I thought I remembered all these things. About Mom. But now...I wonder if I just imagined them." Tears filled her eyes as she stared at the Christmas photo again. If she closed her eyes, she could imagine her mother tying that bow in her hair. Had it never happened? Or had she just stared at this photo enough times to make a story up about it?

"They did all happen," her father insisted. "These photos are just the proof. They captured a moment in time. It was all real. The camera doesn't lie."

Hannah let her eyes drift to another on the pile. Evie on the old tree swing outside. Her hair was a mess and she was wearing pink and white striped pajamas. She must have been about three then, back before Chip got it all together. She smiled, sadly. The camera didn't lie.

"These are for you," Chip said. "And Evie, if she wants them."

Hannah started to shake her head, but her father rested a hand on hers. When she gave him a long, unwilling look, he said, "I don't ask for much. Just...promise me this. Don't let a few bad experiences close you off from the possibility of something wonderful. I'm living proof that some relationships fail. But things have a way of working out the way they were supposed to. Look at all these happy moments. I wouldn't have traded for the world."

"Oh, Dad." Hannah couldn't fight the tears that fell as she leaned in and gave her father a long, hard hug, the smell and feel of him as familiar as all those long, hard hugs he'd given her for so many years.

She pulled back and sniffed. "So we're good?"

"We were always good, Hannah," he said with a wink. "Now, want me to see if Joe can finish up the kitchen instead of Dan?"

Hannah thought about it and then gave a nod. "I think that would be for the best."

Dan had his life. She had hers. And once again, it was time to move forward in separate directions.

*

Evie didn't know whether to laugh or cry half the time these days. She walked back from the beach, guided by the moonlight, knowing she should have accepted Liam's offer to drop her off, but, like all the other nights, she didn't want to raise suspicion with her family. Her father might not directly ask, but Hannah would, and really, what was there to say?

Liam was an editor. She'd gleaned this over the many nights she'd met Liam for picnics on the beach...for a little more on the beach. She stopped to close her eyes, and then quickly opened them again.

Seriously! What had gotten into her? This was crazy. Well, not literally, but damn close to it. Liam was Jack's former editor. He lived in New York. He would be leaving. Soon. As in, this weekend. He'd go back to his life, his successful career. And Evie would...go back to tending bar?

She itched her cheek, and then her chin, thinking at first that she had been bitten by a mosquito, but it was a hive. She could feel them growing, spreading along her jaw line and over her forehead, the evidence of what a mess her life was, inside and out. It wasn't supposed to be this way. But then, so much of life wasn't supposed to be this way, she thought a little sadly.

Liam was...gorgeous. But he was also a distraction. Just like pouring drinks at The Lantern was. It was an excuse that kept her in the safe zone, a place where she didn't have to think about what she really wanted out of life and what she had worked so hard for.

But Liam was also fun. And so was tending bar. And she'd never really known fun, had she? It had been safer to stick to herself, her studies, her aspirations. Those were the things with a guarantee in life.

At least, they were supposed to be.

She was home now, approaching the house, and she walked to the back, careful not to wake anyone. She was just reaching for the handle to the kitchen door when she heard her name whispered in the darkness.

She jumped. Practically screamed, and oh, wouldn't that have given that busybody Beverly something to talk about? Knowing Bev, she'd probably call the police, or come by the next day with a head tilt of faux concern and a hunger in her eyes, asking if everything was okay...

"I didn't mean to scare you," Hannah said. She was sitting on the old swing, the one that still hung from the old tree that centered their backyard. It was so big that their father used to complain it killed the grass. But they loved the shade it provided on hot summer days, and the color the leaves turned every fall.

"You didn't," Evie said. "Well, only a little." With slight reluctance, she walked over to the picnic table and dropped onto it. It felt good. Her feet ached from the walk back to the house.

"I talked to Dad," Hannah said, and Evie was surprised to hear it. She hadn't known Hannah had it in her. God knew she had waited long enough.

But the surprise quickly turned to relief. Relief that Hannah wasn't going to ask about her life. Where she'd been. Who she'd been with. Her time with Liam was coming to an end. It had been wonderful. It was wonderful. But it couldn't last. And it was time for her to start behaving like an adult again.

"I'm sorry, Evie. For everything. For leaving. For seeking out Mom. And Kelly."

Kelly. That was the part that hurt the worst in a way. Kelly. Another sister. But somehow, it felt like her replacement. The sister that *her* sister had spent the last decade bonding with, instead of her. Did she like her better? Was she more fun? Was she the younger sister Hannah always wished she had and had finally found?

Evie sighed. "I understand why you did it. Honestly, I do. But...I have feelings too. And it was just hard for me to not feel, well, forgotten." Threatened was a better word, she knew, but she couldn't bring herself to say it.

"You were never forgotten," Hannah promised, and the firmness of her tone made Evie believe it. She stopped swinging and sighed. "I didn't handle it right. I didn't know how to balance things. A part of me wanted you to want what I wanted. A relationship with Mom."

"I wanted that," Evie said. "But—"

"You knew it would never happen?"

Evie looked at her sadly. The light from the moon was bright enough that she could make out Hannah's expression. She seemed resigned. Defeated. Unlike the Hannah she'd seen just a few days ago, who seemed lighter and happier. More hopeful.

"No, because I was afraid of getting hurt, I guess."

"Oh." Hannah frowned, and the girls sat in silence for a long time. Evie itched her forehead. Then her neck.

"Mosquitoes?"

Evie shook her head. "Hives. Same as the night you came back. Stress. I don't know what I'm doing with my life. I had a plan..."

"Me too," Hannah said with a secret smile. "Guess we have more in common than we thought."

Evie shrugged. "Maybe." She had to admit, she liked the sound of that.

"You're really smart, Evie," Hannah said with a smile. "And you're insightful. You take the time listen to people. I can see why you make such a good therapist."

"I'm just a bartender," Evie grumbled.

"No," Hannah said firmly. "You're not. You help people. I see those poor guys coming into the bar. They need you. Maybe you just need some time to figure out how to help yourself."

Evie thought about this. Maybe. And maybe that was okay, to step back, take some time. She had never really allowed that for herself, had she? She'd been too worried if she stopped, gave herself a break, that everything would come crashing down.

Well, it had. But she was still here. And she'd actually never been happier, she realized. "So you're really going to stay in Oyster Bay?" she asked. "And Dan?"

"Dan and I are over," Hannah said. "We were over a long time ago."

"But—"

"Alicia is back," Hannah said, and Evie knew that there was nothing more to say. She waited to see if

Hannah wanted to talk any more about it, but she'd shut down again, shut off, the way she'd done so easily all those years ago.

Evie considered this for a moment. Thinking of herself, not even trying to get to know her mother or her half-sister. Maybe she was more like Hannah than she'd thought. She'd closed a door without ever walking through it.

"Do you keep in touch with Kelly?" she asked suddenly.

Hannah looked at her in surprise, but her expression turned to one of guilt. "She's reached out to me since I came back. I didn't respond. I felt bad responding. Like I was betraying you and Dad or something."

Evie appreciated that, more than she would say. It was enough, she thought. More than enough. And it was time to start moving forward again.

"If you get in touch with her…maybe you could tell her that I say hi or something?"

Hannah smiled broadly. "I will. She'd…she'd love that, Evie."

The thought of her half-sister—younger sister—caring to hear anything about her was humbling. And shaming. But it was complicated. Life was complicated. And she was exhausted just thinking about it anymore.

"I'm beat," she said, standing and looking toward the back door longingly. "You coming in?"

Hannah shook her head. "I'll be in later. See you in the

morning?"

"Won't you be gone in the morning?" Evie asked, thinking of how Hannah had dashed off every morning since she'd been back, aside from a few days last week.

"Joe's going to finish the kitchen," Hannah replied, and again, that was all Evie needed to know.

They'd both taken a chance. Something they hadn't done in a long time. And now…they'd have to start over. Again.

Only this time they'd be doing it together, Evie thought. And that was something. In fact, it was a lot.

Chapter Seventeen

Just as quickly as Alicia had come back, she was gone again. Dan wasn't sure what surprised him more—that she'd come back at all, or that he was happy that she had. Now there was closure. Now he could stop blaming himself, stop wondering if. If, if, if. His life was so full of hypothetical situations. If he'd never fought with Hannah. If he'd never gone to that party. If he'd never had one too many beers. If he'd tried harder, made more of an effort, really allowed himself to love Alicia.

But half of it was out of his control. Hannah had played her part and Alicia had played hers. And Alicia hadn't loved him either. And now...now the world felt full of possibility, the heavy weight of regret and confusion gone. Alicia had left, but she'd be back to visit. She was moving forward with her life, and he was moving forward with his. It was better this way. Even for Lucy, he now believed. He'd make sure of it.

The only thing still out of his control was, of course, Hannah.

Lucy had mentioned their run-in last weekend. And not surprisingly, Chip had asked if Joe might step in and finish the job, and after only a pause, Dan had agreed. The project would be wrapped up this week, anyway, and it was better for Dan to sort through his home life, keep focused. He had a daughter to think about. It wasn't just his future anymore. It hadn't been for a long time.

Dan hovered on the landing outside Lucy's bedroom door and hesitated before knocking twice. She'd been in there for the last hour, and he'd given her space, knowing that her mother's departure last night hadn't been an easy one, especially when she'd just gotten her back.

He tried the door, relieved to find it unlocked, and opened it carefully, surprised to see his daughter sitting at her desk near the window, drawing in her sketchpad.

He'd half expected her to be lying in bed, crying, maybe even blaming him for Alicia leaving again, the way she had the first time.

"I was thinking of going into town," he said, feeling out the situation. "We're out of milk."

"And ice cream," Lucy said, not looking up from her drawing. It was another mermaid, this one surrounded by starfish.

"Ice cream. Of course. Name your flavor. Name two flavors."

Now Lucy looked up and frowned at him. "Since when do you let me pick out two flavors?"

"Since…" He trailed off. It was the guilt talking. And she was old enough and smart enough to see through it. "I just thought, in case you were sad, that your mom left."

"She'll be back," Lucy said, her voice a little fearful, but firm, as if she was convincing herself, reminding herself that it was true.

In all the time that Alicia was gone, Dan had never promised Lucy that her mother would return. He didn't promise her anything he couldn't be sure of. He still wouldn't.

"She said she'd be back the first weekend of every month," Lucy said, and Dan grinned.

Alicia had changed, for the better, and with a bit of sadness he realized that he liked her a lot more now than he did when they were married. It gave him hope, and it gave him faith. "She told me that too. And if you'd like, one of those weekends you can go stay with her. If you'd like that."

Lucy's eyes popped open and she sprang up from her chair to throw her arms around his neck. Her joy encompassed him, and he closed his eyes, in relief, in happiness, in the silent promise he'd made to her, before he'd ever even met her, when he committed to her, changed his world for her.

"I take it that you're still up for a Spaghetti Saturday?"

he asked hopefully.

"Of course!" Lucy looked at him for a moment. "Maybe Hannah could join us again?"

They hadn't spoken about Hannah since that night. Alicia had returned, and for the week, Lucy could only focus on that. Aside from the passing comment that she'd seen Hannah in town, Lucy seemed to have forgotten her, or at least, shown no interest in her.

Now Dan allowed himself to think of that night again. How right it felt. How complete. "You'd like that?"

Lucy grinned. "I would."

"So would I," he said with relief. He'd like that very much. The only question was, would Hannah?

He stopped Lucy when they got out to the truck. "Just in case she says she can't come, don't feel bad, okay? Sometimes adults decide not to be friends anymore."

"Why wouldn't she want to be your friend?" Lucy asked, her expression folding in confusion. "You still want to be her friend, don't you?"

More than friends, he thought.

*

Hannah walked up to the counter at Angie's and collected her coffee. Make that a frozen confection complete with whipped cream and chocolate shavings. It was cold, decadent, and creamy. And when she was finished, she might just order another.

She was feeling good. Well, maybe not good, but better. She'd emailed Kelly, and mentioned Evie, and tomorrow she and Evie were going to have lunch together, and maybe even do something crazy like go shopping, too. Their bedrooms needed transformations, and neither were in a position to move out of the nest quite yet. She didn't mind living at home a little while longer. If anything, she was almost looking forward for the chance to stay. It would give her a chance to take back some of the years she'd lost.

Or maybe…just misplaced.

She pushed out the door into the sunshine and took a long sip from the straw, contemplating which way to turn. She was working, technically, on assignment to track down a picture of the state insect for an article about, well, the state insects.

She laughed to herself. It wasn't exactly a challenging position, but it was a peaceful one. And besides, it allowed her to do what she loved and where she loved it. Here, in Oyster Bay. The home she'd left once and wouldn't leave again.

Even if she hadn't found everything she'd hoped for in it.

She pushed away the tug in her chest and walked to the corner. The town green always had a carefully landscaped variety of flowers, so she'd stop there before heading home for the day. It was warm and sunny, and the sky was filled with puffy clouds. She should be smiling. She should feel happy at the promise of a relaxing weekend and a lobster bake with Evie and her father tomorrow night. But her heart felt heavy, and she was grateful for the sunglasses that hid the pain that shone in her eyes.

Dan was gone. He was gone a long time ago. She'd accepted that, moved on, and eventually, all those little memories and happy moments they'd shared faded. She'd met new people, dozens of new people, she'd grown and engrossed herself in other activities, places, and things. But all it took was three weeks to feel as if all those moments they'd shared were yesterday. The laughter, the warmth, the sense of security…she'd dared to relive it, cherish it. And now, it was gone. And this time, it almost felt worse. Because this time, it was bittersweet.

Dan was happy. He'd built a good life for himself. And someday, she hoped, she would too.

She crossed the street, into the square, and walked the perimeter, feeling the cool grass under her feet when she toed off her sandals. The state insect was a honeybee, something she should quickly be able to spot, other than the fact that she suddenly realized that there were many types of bees, weren't there?

She sighed in frustration and walked over to a park bench, where she could do a little research on her phone. She hadn't even pulled up the first article when she felt a tap on her shoulder and there, to her horror, stood Beverly Wright.

And Tim.

After an internal eye roll, she gave a polite smile and said, "Hello, Mrs. Wright. Hello, Tim."

"I couldn't help overhearing you talking to your sister the other night," Bev said, her eyes doing this strange little blinking thing that said she was holding back her excitement, or trying to look innocent when she knew she was guilty as hell. Or both.

Hannah frowned. "I didn't realize we were talking so loudly. I'm sorry to have disturbed you."

"Oh, you didn't disturb me," Bev was quick to reply. "But Evie's been coming in so late these days, and that isn't like her, so naturally I was worried..."

"And you went outside to investigate?" Hannah couldn't help herself.

"Well. I...I..." Bev's jaw slacked, and for a moment, Hannah wondered if she would be shamed into walking away. Instead, she pressed her lips together and gave poor Tim a good hard shove. "Timmy has something to ask you."

"I was wondering." He cleared his throat. His face was red, and if Hannah didn't know better, she'd almost say he looked on the verge of tears. Bev's expression, meanwhile, was full of impatience bordering on fury.

Hannah felt bad. She shouldn't have said that to Bev. Now Bev would take her frustration out on Tim.

"I was wondering." Tim took a deep breath. When he released it, it shook.

"He's wondering if you're free for dinner tonight," Bev all but snapped. Then, composing herself, she tipped her head and smiled sweetly. "We all know about Alicia's return this week," she said quietly.

"Then you'll know that she left again. It was a wonderful visit for Lucy. She really enjoyed having that time with her mother," a voice said, and Hannah stiffened at the sight of Dan, who was smoothly approaching the bench, hands in the pockets of his chinos, his jaw hard, but when he looked over at her, his eyes kind.

Hannah barely registered the lump that seemed to wedge in Bev's throat, or the stammered excuses she made as she hurried off, her hand firm on Tim's elbow. All she could think was that Dan was here. He was here. And Alicia wasn't.

Dan stopped a few feet from the bench. "Mind if I sit with you for a moment?"

"I was just leaving," Hannah replied.

"Please—" he said, stopping her. "I know you're not speaking to me. I know I should have…told you. Myself. But I'm here now. And I'm asking for a chance. One more chance."

One more chance. A few minutes ago she hadn't even thought that was possible, and now, suddenly everything was. She looked up at him, into the eyes of the boy she had loved, and the man he had become, and she knew that she couldn't say no even if she wanted to. Dan was her past. Her youth, her dream. And maybe, if she dared to believe it, he could be her future.

"Okay then," she said. Her heart was beating quickly as he slowly sat down beside her, so close that his thigh skimmed hers. She had the urge to slide to the left, shift away, but that would be like pushing away an old friend. And for what? For doing the right thing? She couldn't fault him. Even if it would have been oh so much easier if she could.

She followed his gaze, over to the gazebo, where Lucy was twirling in the center, her sundress circling around her, her arms wide.

"She seems happy," Hannah observed, smiling at the sight.

"She is," Dan said. He licked his bottom lip, his brow was pensive. Finally he looked at her. "I wasn't sure she would be. When Alicia left again."

"What do you mean by left again?" Hannah asked carefully. Selfishly, she wanted Alicia gone, forever. But for Lucy's sake...for the little girl in her who hadn't known her own mother, she hoped like hell that Alicia would be back again.

"Alicia and I are over," Dan said. "But this time away...in a way, it was needed. Alicia's in a better place, and I guess that I am too. She wants to be a part of Lucy's life and I want that for her. For now, that will mean visits, hopefully on a regular basis, and...an open door."

Hannah nodded, trying to process all this information. "And you're okay with that?"

Dan nodded. "I want to be friends with Alicia. For Lucy's sake. What we had before...it wasn't fair to any of us."

Hannah swallowed. She wanted to believe that it could all be this easy, that there was a space in Dan's life for her. A place in his heart. But she still felt cut out, excluded. "Why didn't you tell me? When my dad asked Joe to finish the kitchen, you must have known that I knew Alicia was back."

"I did," Dan agreed. "Lucy told me that she ran into you. I wanted to talk to you. I wanted to explain. But first...I needed to deal with things at home. I needed to make sure that this time, I had closure."

"And do you?" Hannah watched him carefully, looking for a hint of doubt in his eyes, but there was none. They were just the same, steady, solid, warm eyes that she'd looked into day after day, for years.

"I was afraid to move on," he said. "I was afraid to let go. I was afraid of messing up Lucy's life the way I'd messed up...Well."

She knew what he'd meant to say. The way he'd messed up his own. Only he hadn't, had he?

"You did what you had to do, and I did what I had to do," she said, offering him a little smile. "I needed to see what would happen in California. I needed that time to chase something that couldn't be found. But now I know."

"And I needed that time to be a father. I wouldn't trade it for the world," he said, looking at her plainly.

"I know," she said, brushing away a tear. "And I never asked you to."

"I keep thinking, how it might have been. If you'd

stayed. If I hadn't married Alicia."

"Don't think that way," Hannah said firmly. "We both made our choices."

"And now we have another choice." He lifted an eyebrow, his grin curving his mouth. "Do we try again?"

"Oh, Danny," Hannah said. Her heart was bursting. She wanted to say, yes, yes, of course, yes! She wanted to scream it and shout it and fling her arms around him and hold him and never let him go.

But she couldn't deny what they'd been through. What they'd loss. A loss they shared, perhaps.

"It was always you, Hannah," Dan said. "I tried to forget you. I did even manage to forget you. But having you back here, it just reminded me, how it was. How it could still be."

He took her hand, squeezed it hard enough to show her that he wasn't going to release it, even if she tried to pull away, which she didn't. His hand was large, warm, and oh so wonderful.

"I'd like that," she said. "I want that too."

"Oh, God! Two old people holding hands on a park bench! Disgusting!" Lucy suddenly shouted from the gazebo, and Dan and Hannah burst into laughter together.

Hannah looked around, wondering if Mimi and Earl had returned, but the green was empty aside from them, and she realized, with a strange awareness, that the people Lucy was referring to were them. As they were. As they could be. Two "old people" holding hands on a park bench.

Some things did last forever.

Lucy marched over to them, her arms folded across her chest. "It's okay to kiss her, Dad. I know how these things work, you know." She rolled her eyes in exaggeration, but she was fighting off a smile.

"I need time to slow down," Dan said, looking at Hannah in alarm.

She grinned as he leaned in to kiss her. "So do I. And this time, we have all the time in the world."

Coming Soon

THOSE SUMMER NIGHTS

Licensed therapist Evie Donovan's life plan was simple: work hard, stay focused, and everything would fall into place. Losing her dream job and having a summer fling were never part of that plan. Now, regrouped and recharged, she is ready to try again, and that means leaving behind the bartending job at her father's restaurant and saying goodbye to those magical (and extremely uncharacteristic) romantic summer nights.

Writing an "Ask Evie" column for the local newspaper is the perfect transition to get her back on track. But her plan didn't include the possibility of her summer fling turning into her permanent boss, or that the black and white world she has chosen to live in is turning a little grey.

Between fantasizing about her now off-limits boss and fielding emails from a half sister she's never met, Evie begins to wonder if she can turn the helpful advice she's known for onto herself. She's used to letting her head be her guide, but for once, she might just be forced to follow her heart—even if it takes her a little off her carefully chosen path...

OLIVIA MILES writes feel-good women's fiction and heartwarming contemporary romance that is best known for her quirky side characters and charming small town settings. She lives just outside Chicago with her husband, young daughter, and two ridiculously pampered pups.

Olivia loves connecting with readers. Please visit her website at www.OliviaMilesBooks.com to learn more.

Made in the USA
Lexington, KY
26 October 2018